MW01615589

THE OTHER SIDE OF THE WALL

BY

MARY E. ROPES

Cover Illustration by Dan Burr
Cover Design by Phillip Colhouer
First Published in 1826
Originally Titled *Jacques Hamon*
This unabridged version has updated grammar and spelling.
© 2019 Jenny Phillips
www.thegoodandthebeautiful.com

To
Freddy and Johnny,
The Little Men
To Whom She Owes Some of the Best and Happiest
Hours of Her Life,
This Book Is Gratefully Dedicated
By Their Loving
"Aunt Weedy"

Contents

Chapter One

Sir Philip States the Case

"I say, Jack! Jersey Jack! Where are you? What—in bed? Why, you lazy lubber! Here's Sir Philip and the French Marquis inquiring after your health."

"All right—I'm awake—I'm coming," I said. "You'd be sleepy too, Ben Tivett, if you'd been up half the night setting the yacht right after such a voyage as we had from Sark."

As quickly as I could, I washed my face and hands, got into my clothes, and brushed my hair. I was not long about it either, for in two minutes by my watch, I was standing in the doorway of the saloon—as pretty a little cabin as you'll ever see, all fitted up according to Sir Philip's own ideas, which were good ones—always.

My master, Sir Philip Penreath, and his friend, the French Marquis de Quedrennes, were sitting at the saloon table, side by side, and spread out before them was a map and some papers.

"Yes, Sere Pheelp, dis is the place where lie the estates of my late cousin," the Marquis was saying as he pointed to a corner of the map near the Breton coastline. "His half-nephew, wid a young wife, live there at the château and have been occupied with the old man's affairs."

Then the Marquis looked up and saw me, and said—

"*Bonjour*, Jacques Hamon."

"*Bonjour*, Monsieur le Marquis," I said.

"Good morning, Jack," said my master. "Come in, will you, my man? And shut the door, please. So—now we can't be overheard on deck. There's a little bit of business on hand—difficult business, and delicate, too—rather, and when we were talking it over, the Marquis and I, and wondering whom we could get to help us, I thought of my trusty sailor, Jersey Jack."

I felt myself getting very hot and red at this, but I didn't mind it, considering the cause. "Thank you kindly, Sir Philip," I said, for of course I was proud to be trusted, and I liked my master to call me Jersey Jack, too, for he only does that when he's in his best mood. Other times it's Jacques, or Jacques Hamon, for I'm a Channel Island man and have a French name, though I've lived in England so long that I've forgot my *patois* and have come to talk English like my mates on the yacht.

"Will you explain the matter to Jack, Marquis, or shall I?" said Sir Philip.

"If you shall be so amiable, mine friend, I will be moche oblige," said the French gent, in that odd lingo of his, which he'd never bettered though he'd been years in England.

"Well, my lad," said my master as he turned to me, "the case is this. The Marquis has just heard of the death of an old gentleman, a cousin of his, in Brittany."

"Yes, Sir Philip," I said, wondering what the death of the old Frenchman had to do with me.

"The deceased gentleman was not married," continued my master. "His name was Pierre de St. Rémy. Some years ago, he made a will—wrote it himself, for he hated lawyers and mistrusted them— in favor of a distant relation of his named Eustache Delmaine, to whom he had always been much attached. This young man and his newly-married wife live in a château on the estates which now, when the will is proved, *should* come into his own possession."

"Ah *dame oui!*" put in the Marquis. "Yes, you say true; and all would be so easy, but for dat *scélérat*—what you call scoundrel— Paul de St Rémy. How wicked is dis world!"

"This Paul de St Rémy," went on Sir Philip, "is own nephew to the deceased, and but for the will that has been made, he would inherit the whole of the property, for he is the only near relation living. But old Pierre long ago learned what manner of man was this nephew of his. Paul had been an idle, dissipated youth and had made his friends thoroughly ashamed of him from the first. Later on, he led the life of an adventurer; he went to Paris and worked during the time of the Revolution as a spy of Robespierre's. Now, like many of that gang, he is employed by Bonaparte in the same sort of dirty work, though he is called a coast guard official. I am right in telling this much, am I not, Marquis?"

"But, certainly," said the Marquis. "Dere is nothing too bad as you can say for Paul de St Rémy. Please to continue, Sere Pheelp."

So my master went on, "Old Pierre de St Rémy, being a shrewd and far-seeing man, was sure that at his death his will would stand a great chance of being destroyed by his nephew Paul, unless special precautions were taken. For, of course, if no papers could be produced, Paul would naturally succeed to the property. So, to make all safe, the old man prepared and signed a duplicate of his will and sent it over to England, to the care of his friend and cousin, the Marquis, whom he could trust to produce it when needful."

"Yes, Sir Philip," I said, as my master stopped a moment. "That's all plain enough, but I don't see yet where I come in."

"I'm coming to that, Jack. Eustache Delmaine writes that already Paul is bestirring himself in the matter of his uncle's property, giving out everywhere that the old gentleman died without a will, and that he—Paul—is therefore the heir to all. In fact, the Marquis learned that he has even applied to the law courts, to put him in possession of his uncle's estate."

"Ah *oui!* What a bad man! Alas! Alas!" said the Marquis in a whisper to himself.

"Are you following, Jack?" said my master.

"Yes, Sir Philip," I said; and so I was—honor bright.

"Eustache Delmaine writes, therefore, to the Marquis, begging him to lose no time in sending his copy of the will to be proved in court. The duplicate copy was left among the old man's papers, and so we may feel sure that, for his own sake, Monsieur Paul has destroyed it."

"But maybe he won't know that there's a copy here, Sir Philip," I said.

"Yes, he would, Jack," said my master. "In the will that the Marquis has just shown me is a note to the effect that a copy is to be found in the old gentleman's safe. There can be little doubt that in this paper—the one left in the safe, I mean—is a similar note, stating that the duplicate is in the possession of the Marquis de Quedrennes, in England. Indeed, Jack, Monsieur Paul de St Rémy *must* know, for the Marquis hears that the château and its neighborhood are being watched by the coast guards. Why should this be, except to intercept any special messenger, the bearer of the will?"

All of a sudden I saw what the master was driving at, and I said, "A messenger, Sir Philip? Ah, now, I understand. It's me you want to send with that paper."

But before Sir Philip had time to answer, up hopped the little Marquis, trembling.

"Ah, *mon garçon!*" he screamed out in his little cracked voice. "I would give dis right hand to be mine own messenger to France. But, *malheureusement*, I shall only lose my life if I land mineself in my country, and Eustache Delmaine loses also de will. It is not secret, Jacques Hamon, dat I left France—*moi*—when de Revolution broke out; and now to return, dis is impossible, if I submit not mineself to Napoleon. Bah!" And up went the little Marquis' big nose in the air. "Shall indeed a royalist and one of *de haute noblesse* do de homage to de Corsican adventurer? *Non! Mille fois non, merci beaucoup! Jamais! Jamais! À bas l'Empereur! Vive le roi et la haute noblesse!*"

The Marquis had gotten to his feet on to the chair, being quite excited. He waved his arms like a windmill and screamed so loudly that I was afraid the sailors would hear. But Sir Philip, he took hold of one arm and said soothingly and gently, "My good friend, this is all very natural. But remember, there is work at hand, and we have no time to lose."

The poor little French gentleman dropped to his seat like a jack-in-the-box with a broken spring.

"You have reason, Sere Pheelp," he said, so meek and humble

that I felt quite sorry for him. "Please have de goodness to proceed, and tell Jacques what he must do."

"But, first, Sir Philip," I said, "how am I to get across the channel?"

"In the way you're best used to, my lad," said my master, smiling. "We'll all go off for a cruise in the *Swift*, and we will contrive to land you somewhere on the coast, not too far from the château. Wild and rocky and very lonely a great part of the Breton shore is—so, Marquis, I think you've told me?"

"Yes, Sere Pheelp, steeped cliffs wid holes in dem and de tide rushing in and out like a horse race."

"Rather a favorite neighborhood with smugglers, I've heard," said Sir Philip. "You ought to know something about that, Jack, for you hail from Jersey, and it's between the Channel Islands and the Breton and Norman coasts that the trade is busiest."

"Yes, Sir Philip," I answered, "I know as much about smuggling as an honest man may."

"Well now, my man," said my master, "if the wind's fair, we must get the *Swift* to sea tonight. It will be sharp work, as we have only just come in, and after heavy weather too. The boat must be made taut and trim. Is the sailing master aboard this morning?"

"I don't know, sir," I answered. "He may be now."

"Well, you had better go and see, Jack," said Sir Philip. "And if he has come, just ask him to step into my private cabin. And the steward had better come to me directly. Mr. Morton leaves the cabin, for he will have to buy provisions at once. And, Jack, just look at the big gun, will you? And see that all's in working order. We may want it, though I hope we shall not. An English yacht—a clipper such as ours—would be a prize worth taking, and in war time she isn't safe from those rascally privateers. We must be all aboard and ready to sail about eight o'clock tonight. The tide will be on the turn, and before nine we'll weigh anchor and let her drop down with the ebb. Now, Marquis," added the master, turning to the little French gent who was sitting in the brownest of all brown studies, "you'd better, please, go home, and pack your valise. Get your best sea legs on, pluck up heart, and be ready to sail tonight. Of course, if you prefer, we can manage the business without you, but I would rather have you with us; you know the coast and can advise where it will be safest to land and what and whom to avoid."

"*Mais certainement,* I shall go wid you," said the Marquis, and up went his head. He straightened out his back, and for a minute, with that proud smile on his face, he looked like the gallant little officer I'd heard he used to be.

"You'll see that things are put in train at once, Jack, please," said Sir Philip, as I opened the cabin door. "Send Mr. Morton first, and tell the steward I want him directly after. And as for yourself, my lad, you'd perhaps better tell your friends that it's possible you may not be back for a week or two. And if you've a sweetheart, why, say a goodbye that will give her something to think about till you come home again."

"Thank you, Sir Philip," I replied, "but I've got nothing of the sort. When I was a youngster, I lost my heart to a little French lass down in Jersey, and I've never thought of no one since."

"*Ma foi!* But dat is constancy!" said the Marquis. "Not too moche French blood in you, Jacques Hamon, dat is very plain! Dis so obstinate love is a fault dat is English only."

"Just one word more, Jack," said my master, as I stood with the door in my hand. "It would be wrong for us to conceal from you that there may be risk in this service which we are asking you to undertake for us. Now, if you shrink from it, say so, and I will make another arrangement—send someone else, or even try to deliver the will myself. There is almost nothing I would not do to prevent Monsieur Pierre's property from falling into the hands of that rascally nephew of his. The Marquis has been my friend for years, and in this matter we are quite as one about what ought to be done."

"I tank you grateful, Sere Pheelp," said the Marquis. "I could do noting at all widout you."

"Well, Jack, now you know there is risk, what say you?" asked my master.

"Just what I said before, Sir Philip," I said. "I've not thought about risk, so please don't *you*. I'll do all I know to keep out of danger, but if I get into a hobble, well—I'll get out the best I can. And, anyhow, please don't think of giving the commission to anyone else, for, risk or no risk, I'm your man!" And with those words for my last, out I went and shut the cabin door.

That night we were up with our anchor a bit before nine, and as the tide began to go out, we went with it, having a fair wind and smooth water. I looked up at the bright moon and clear stars. As we got out to sea, I said to myself, standing at the helm, "What'll happen, I wonder, before we come sailing in, as now we're sailing out! God only knows," I said, "but anyway, it's a comfort that God *does* know."

Chapter Two

In the Dead of Night

I suppose the gales had blown themselves out, finishing up with the big storm we'd been fighting with on that passage from Sark that I've spoken of already. Anyhow, there never was finer weather than we started with, and kept, too, all the way across the channel. We had a good breeze, too, but it was fair, and the *Swift* went flying away before it, like the swallow she was named for.

There wasn't any motion to speak of, at least not for anyone at all used to the sea, and Sir Philip didn't take any notice of it. But the Marquis couldn't come on deck till late in the morning after our start, and when he did turn up, his poor little pinched face had nearly as many colors as a rainbow.

"Ah, Jacques," he said to me as I got him a camp-stool and rugs and made him comfortable in a sheltered corner. "Ah, Jacques, *le mal de mer, c'est la mère des maux, n'est-ce pas, mon garçon?*" And, truly, it seemed as if his being sea-sick had doubled all his troubles, and they'd been neither few nor small before—poor little gentleman!

We had no adventures worth mentioning till we were nearing the Breton coast, and the great wild rocks and cliffs and islands stood out against the clear sky in the distance for all the world like a lovely picture.

It was afternoon, and as Sir Philip said there was no thought of landing me before dark, he gave Mr. Morton orders to run down the coast at a safe distance from the shore. Mr. Morton was to keep an eye open for any little quiet bay or lonely nook that would make a good place to run a boat into later on.

Under the land here the sea was quite smooth, and the Marquis began to be nice and lively, hopping about all over the deck, glass in hand, looking out for the different points he knew as we sailed along.

"Ah, yes," he said, "dere's St. Malo, wid de big wall and de islands round. For me to land mineself here shall cost me mine head. And opposite is lovely Dinard, and, *plus loin*, round de corner, is de sunny bay of Paramé. I did play on dose sand when I was leetle child and catched shrimp in di pools of rock. Ah! How dose days are long time past!" And the poor Marquis' bright face went into puckers all in a minute, like a child's, and he gave a little sob. He was so ashamed of the sob that he turned it into a cough and finished up by blowing a blast on his great nose; then he cheered up and was quite himself afterwards.

We were still quietly gliding along under about half as much sail as the yacht usually carried when we spied a smallish vessel, lying rather low in the water and top-heavy with canvas, following us. Sir Philip and Mr. Morton stood together with their glasses up, and now they looked around at each other and said at the same moment, "Privateer!"

"But we don't care about being overtaken just yet," said my master, smiling. "We must not come to close quarters with any craft till our work's done, for if we were recognized, the work might be made doubly hard for us. So please, Mr. Morton, give orders to our men to crowd on sail, and we'll show this fellow a clean pair of heels."

The order was given, the great white wings were spread, and away over the dancing blue fled the *Swift*, well deserving her name as she sped on with a brisk side wind. The privateer followed for a bit, but presently, whether seeing that her speed was no match for ours or spying in the distance an English frigate cruising about, blockading the ports on that coast, she made for a creek and disappeared behind a big rocky island.

It was evening and fast getting dark before the orders were given to about ship and run back, the side wind still serving us in good stead.

Sir Philip, the Marquis, and the sailing-master had among
'em settled on the place where a little boat might land me and the
precious will, which was sewed and sealed up in some waterproof
stuff and tucked safe away in an inner pocket of my vest, under the
seaman's jersey that I always wear.

The quiet little nook where I was to land lay under an
overhanging cliff, into which a cave burrowed. At night it would still
be highish tide and deep water, so the boat could pull close in. Right
from the shore a pathway led zigzagging up the cliff, coming out at
the top into a thick copse of young trees and brushwood, this copse
belonging to the very estate of the late Monsieur Pierre de St Rémy.

If I found I was able to land here without anyone seeing me, it
ought not to be hard to find my way, under cover of the night, to the
château. Confident as those with little experience often are, I said to
myself, "This ain't going to be much of a job after all!"

It was past midnight before we sailed back far enough to get
opposite the place, and now orders were given to cast anchor and
get out the small boat. While the orders were being carried out, Sir
Philip called me into the cabin where the Marquis was too.

He said, "Jack, my boy, you don't need to be told how much
depends upon you this night. Neither of us doubt for one moment
your faithfulness or your courage, and I am sure that, for the sake of
all concerned—yourself included—you will also be prudent."

"You may count on my doing all that a man may, Sir Philip.
I can't say more!" And no more I could, for a big lump formed
in my throat, my master's words being so kind and his dear face
kinder still.

Then the Marquis hopped up in his wonderful Jack-in-the-box
style, and he said, "*Le bon Dieu* go wid you, Jacques Hamon, and
give you succeed, and send speedy your home return. I tank you,
mon brave garçon, and it is not me dat will forget de reward when
you came back."

"Try to remember all the instructions you have received, Jack,"
said Sir Philip. "And when you have safely delivered your basket,
bear in mind that the signal we have agreed upon is a flare shown

for one instant only on the rocky ledge halfway up the cliff, just opposite where we are lying now. This is, of course, a night-signal only, and I fear it is too much to expect that you should do your errand and be back and signaling to us before the morning breaks. But we cannot attempt to send a boat for you by daylight; the risk would be too great. So, even if you are through with what you have to do by tomorrow morning, you must lie close, either at the château, or hidden in the copse, till dark."

"I quite understand, Sir Philip," I said, "and I won't forget."

"Then, once more, goodbye and God bless you," said my master.

He followed me up on deck and looked down over the ship's side while I got into the boat. Then we pushed off and went stealing out into the darkness, toward the lonely shore.

The oars were muffled, and the two men rowing said never a word save in whispers, for such were our orders.

But just as we'd got halfway towards the place we were steering for, I saw something that sent the heart up into my mouth, as the saying is. The men, having their backs to the shore, rowing, could see nothing, but I was at the rudder; and what startled me was nothing more nor less than a sudden flash of light, right in the very mouth of the dark cave that opened up like a tunnel under the cliff in front.

"Easy all!" I whispered, and the men lay on their oars.

"What is it, Jack?" said stroke, leaning forward and looking at me anxiously.

"A sudden light, Ben; it just flashed and were gone," I said.

"Whereabouts?" asked bow.

"Right inside the cave," I said, "close by where I'm to land."

"Shall we turn and row back to the yacht?" whispered Ben.

"No," I said. "I'll see this through, now that I have started out. Pull on for another minute or two, mates, till we gets a little nearer. Softly now, don't splash! A little noise can be heard a long way on the water, such a night as this." For in the truth, the wind had dropped now to a mere breath, and the waves crept up to the shore with scarce more than a murmur.

The men pulled on, silent and swift, for maybe three minutes more, then I gave them the order to stop.

"Just dip your oars to hold her and keep her from drifting," I said. Then I stood up and took my coat and big, heavy sailor's boots off.

"Why, Jack, what are you after?" said Ben, looking as if he thought I'd gone mad.

"I'm going to swim to the landing place," I said. "You see, mates, that light shows there must be folks on the watch for something, and a boat would be seen if she came at all near. But I can get there swimming easy enough, and if they were to turn the light on again, I can dive and swim underwater a bit. Now I'm going overboard, boys, just here, and as soon as you see me come up and strike out fair for the shore, you row back to the yacht and tell the master all about it. Say to him and the Marquis, from Jersey Jack, that by hook or by crook, somehow or other, I hope to do the work I'm sent for, if my life's spared."

Then I shook hands with my mates and slipped into the sea, making no splash, and struck out for the dark line of the shore. The water wasn't very cold, for we'd had a warmer summer than common, with a lot of sunshine, and these were still the early days of September. So, I'd no cramps and did my swimming quite comfortably, now treading water, now cutting along with the swift side stroke, but always careful not to get my head too high so as to be seen.

As I came nearer the shore, I could make things out much more clearly. There was the cave, looking like a great, black yawning mouth, set in the face of the rugged cliff, and there, too, was the pathway—of a lighter color—running in a winding, zigzagging, terracing sort of fashion, up to the top. To the right of the cave, as I faced it, there was a big boulder standing high out of the water. I said to myself, "That's where I must land, for no one can see me behind that." So I kept well to the right, and presently my feet touched bottom. In another moment I was scrambling out behind the rock. But do what I would to be quiet, one or two loose stones rolled over and splashed into the water, and again I saw the light flash out for an instant as I peeped around my friend the boulder. If I'd been in the water opposite the cave that minute, I must have been seen. Providentially, I was hidden. But, lying there like a hare in her form, I heard muttering close by me in the cave.

"What was that noise, Jean?" said a deep gruff voice in the bad French the folks speak in these parts.

"Nothing at all," said a thin, piping voice, which I suppose was the man Jean's. "You are always expecting and fancying danger, Simon."

"While you, for your part, keep no lookout at all," said the gruff-voiced Simon.

"And what need of always watching and listening? Does not *le maître* do that for us?" said Jean with a yawn.

The talk of the two men went on in low tones, but I didn't stop to listen no more. I stepped softly from behind the boulder and began to mount the narrow path leading to the cliff top.

I must have climbed about halfway up when I came to the ledge the Marquis had told us of, and where I was to show my flare when my work was done and I was ready to be taken off again to the yacht.

The ledge was a fairly broad one, from five to six feet, I should say, and over it the rock had made a kind of roof. It was just as if a great lump out of the middle of the corner of cliff had broken away from the mass, leaving a top and a bottom, and so making a roof and a floor. The pathway was a step or two below the ledge and just there turned sharp to go from left to right in its zigzag up the cliff.

I was standing here for a moment, getting my breath, when I heard footsteps coming light and quick down the path above me. I'd no time to think, but it was instinct maybe that made me clamber up to the ledge, drawing myself well back into the deep shadow of the rock roof. Here I stood, hardly daring to breathe. The steps came nearer, nearer still; they turned the corner made by the sharp turn of the path, and in a moment they were just in front of me. The man that belonged to the footsteps was a tall man, wrapped up in a long cloak. He seemed to walk slower somehow as he passed my perch on the ledge. Would he look up? Would he see me if he did? Just below—lower on the slope of the pathway, I mean—the man stood still a moment and looked down over the cliff. Then he moved on, and I gave a big gasp, like a half-drowned man that gets his lungs full of air again.

"Where can he be going?" I said to myself. "And what to do?"

Then, feeling strongly that somehow he and the other men in the cave might be mixed up with the business I had on hand, and the one could hardly know too much of what was going on so near the château, I stepped down from the ledge. Making not a sound with my socked feet, I followed the man down, only just keeping him in sight, though, in case he should turn and spy me.

Well, down, down he went to the very bottom. I saw his tall figure slip by the boulder where I'd hidden and then disappear into the cave.

I couldn't follow him there, but it might be worth a lot to me to know what this meeting meant, and if any fresh mischief were afoot. So I set about to hunt for someplace where I could overhear what was said without going to my first station behind the boulder, which was nearer than I cared to be again, if I'd had my choice. But all my hunting and searching were for nothing. There was no choice in the matter. Either I must take up my old place or give up the idea of knowing what it was that those three could be doing in a lonely cave, in the dead of night.

"Hobson's choice!" I said to myself, and, with a passing pity for Hobson, who always seemed to get the worst of everything, I stole down and planted myself on the seaward side of the boulder.

The water had ebbed a good bit so that I now stood on dry, soft sand. I'd hardly settled myself there before I heard Simon's big voice grumbling:

"You have kept us long, *mon maître*. Now we have hardly time to put the stuff in safely before daylight."

And then came the answer in hard, clear tones, like a blow on bell metal, and I could hear every word, though the voice wasn't raised at all.

"If I have kept you waiting, Simon and Jean, it has not been without reason. I have many things to see to just now. But you still have time. If you begin the work at once, you can make the transfer safely, for I have drawn off the coast guard from this neighborhood and set them to watch elsewhere."

"Then we are to begin at once, Maître Paul?" said Jean's voice.

"At once," he answered.

"And there is no danger?" growled Simon.

"Bah! Always danger!" said Jean.

"Danger?" said Maître Paul. "No, how can there be? There is not a soul within a mile of us. Have I not just come down the cliff myself, and should I not have seen had there been anyone?

"Now, make haste, my men—move the things from the back of this cave up to the barn behind my house. The side door is open, and you can get in easily. This time the packages are not large, nor are they many, so they will not take long to move. Tobacco is so much lighter than English goods. I will await you there and receive the stuff myself."

"But, *mon maître*, we want something on account," said Simon.

"True, I forgot," said Maître Paul. Then I heard money chinking, and I knew Maître Paul would be out in a minute. So down I go on my knees in the sand, scraping it up all around me, drawing the great tangles of seaweed that hung from the boulder on the seaward side over my head and shoulders. It wasn't likely he would pass on this side as he left the cave, but he might take a look around, and if he did, all he'd see would be a heap of sand and weed washed up around the big stone by the late tide.

Another moment and Maître Paul passed, and before the men had time to come with their packages, I slipped out. Once more following at a distance and under cover of the thick night, I watched Maître Paul pass like a black specter through the copse and, turning to the left, come out into a little open space with a small house and a building behind it, which I suppose was the barn. Then I crept back into the copse, right to the other side of it, away from the path which the men would take toward Maître Paul's house.

One thing was plain; these men were smugglers. And as for

Maître Paul—why, he was a smuggler too, or a receiver of the goods, which was just as bad.

Somewhere or other—years ago—I had heard that man's voice. I may forget a face, but never a voice, and his was not one hard to remember. Now, how and where did I hear it? "Ah! I have it!" I said to myself. "It was at Jersey, when by chance I came upon that gang loading their boat on the sly. This chap was giving them their orders. Ah! Then, Maître Paul was a smuggler then as now. But what was it he said about the coast guard? That he had set them to watch elsewhere? He? Then he must be in command over the coast guards—and if—no—could it be? Yet the name, too, corresponding—? Yes, that's it! There can be no mistake about it. Maître Paul's a smuggler. Maître Paul is commander of the coast guard here, and last, but not least—Maître Paul is the spy, the traitor, the cowardly cheat and swindler—Monsieur Paul de St Rémy."

And just as I'd worked this out to full satisfaction in my own mind, I found myself at the gate of a shrubbery, through which there led a long, dark, winding pathway bordered with lumps of rock, with green things and wildflowers growing between them. Then the narrow path came suddenly to an end, and the château, in the midst of a garden, was before me. The moon came out for the first time that night from the clouds, making the whole beautiful place as light almost as day.

Chapter Three

I Deliver up My Trust

As I stood there looking around and peering under the shadow of the trees, just to make quite sure that no one was about, the stillness was almost painful. The soft rustle of a dry leaf or two among the evergreens, and the gentle, sleepy drone of the ripples far down below on the beach were all I could hear. Notwithstanding, I looked and listened my best (and I had sharp enough eyes and ears, too). There was nobody to be seen nor yet heard. "A precious good thing for me, and a precious bad one for himself," I said with an inward chuckle, "that Maître Paul didn't know what he was doing—or failing to do—when he ordered the coast guard off the shore and the copse, to make the smuggling work easy. But now, for the sake of a few bales or boxes of contraband stuff, he's letting what's a thousand times more precious slip through those swindler's fingers of his. But that's often the way with these clever scamps; there are times when they're too clever and overreach themselves."

I daresay Maître Paul had never thought of any messenger from England landing in such a little out-of-the-way place as this, and maybe, too, the *Swift*, having made a very quick passage, was earlier than he'd expected.

But, whichever way it were, here I was. Now, having satisfied myself that the garden wasn't occupied by anyone but myself, I stepped up to the front door and looked up at the windows. They were all dark save one, but in that one a bright light was shining, and the shadow of a man kept coming and going on the white blind.

A goat's foot hanging from a chain seemed to be the only bell there was. I took hold, gave it a pull, and heard a faint tinkle far away somewhere inside the house; a great dog barked at the same time.

I waited maybe about three minutes. Then a quick footstep sounded inside, and a little sliding panel in the door slipped back.

A voice said in French, "Who is it?"

"A messenger from England," I whispered.

"Your name, if you please?"

"Jacques Hamon, able sailor onboard the yacht *Swift*."

"And from whom come you?"

"From Monsieur le Marquis de Quedrennes and Sir Philip Penreath, his friend."

The bolts slid back; the key turned in the lock. The door opened.

"Enter, if you please," said a pleasant voice.

I stepped in and looked up quick to see, by the light of the candle that he who questioned me was holding, if the face agreed with the voice. It didn't take long to make up my mind about that. I thought, as I glanced at Monsieur Eustache Delmaine (for I couldn't have a doubt it were him), that it was no wonder old Monsieur Pierre de St Rémy was so fond of this half-nephew of his and left him his property. The thought of the property gave me a reminder of the precious packet I was carrying, and I said in a whisper, "Monsieur, I have something for you from Monsieur le Marquis."

"Come in here, if you please," he said, and I followed him into a sort of study or library; at least, there was a writing table and lots of books and papers.

"Pray, be seated," said Monsieur Delmaine, pointing to an easy chair. But as he did this, it struck me all of a sudden for the first time that I was hardly in a state to come into a gentleman's house at all, much less to sit down on a chair that had red and white roses growing—as it seemed—all over the seat, and other flowers, such as I knew nothing about, twining and climbing up the cushioned back.

Well, I looked at the chair, then I looked down at myself, and I saw a dirty, dripping scarecrow of a sailor: no coat, no boots, socks cut through in a dozen places. My jersey and trousers were covered in wet sand and odds and ends of broken shell and seaweed, and to make this lovely picture complete, I was holding in my hand (for I had doffed it as I came in) a limp blue wool rag that called itself a knitted cap once. Yes—for a special courier, sent by a French Marquis and an English Baronet, it couldn't be denied but that I might have been better dressed and a trifle cleaner.

So, having looked myself all over, I finished by glancing up at the young gentleman and said, laughing heartily, "Pardon, Monsieur, I have sins enough to answer for without spoiling your furniture. But if you could see what I have been doing tonight since I left Sir Philip's yacht over there in the offing, you would not wonder at my strange appearance. But now, Monsieur, permit me to hand over to your safe keeping the parchment which I came to bring." And I drew out the waterproof basket from my vest pocket and put it into his hands.

Then, as he opened the packet, I sat down (on a wooden chair—not on that horticultural show) and watched him. And never—saving always and of course my own dear master's, God bless him, did I see any face like it for winning love, so strong and yet so sweet. For the rest, he was a tall man—as tall as that scoundrel, Maître Paul, but broader in the shoulder and deeper in the chest, seeming firmer set up altogether, I should say.

It didn't take Monsieur Delmaine long to glance through the will. Then he folded it again, slipped it into his pocket, and said, "Tomorrow morning, my good Jacques Hamon, I shall ask you to tell me your story, but now you must have dry clothes, supper, and bed. What orders have you received about rejoining your vessel?"

"I cannot get on board, Monsieur, until tomorrow night—tonight I mean," I said, glancing up at the clock, which pointed to a quarter past three.

"Follow me, Jacques," said Monsieur, and he led the way into a kitchen where there was still a lot of hot water in the boiler. A big tin basin and some soap was in the sink under a cold-water tap, and Monsieur Delmaine brought me a towel. Then he went away and came back almost directly with some flannel clothing, a pair of socks, and stout shoes.

"Now," he said, "wash and change, and then return to my study, and you can sleep there on the couchette."

Oh, what a joy it was to get off the sticky, clinging, sea-watery clothes and put on dry, warm ones! Then, when I went back to the study, there was a nice little supper put out for me on the table. Monsieur Delmaine had prepared it for me himself. Yes, too much of a gentleman he was to think such things beneath his dignity. It's only your snob that's always on the lookout in case he should do something not quite up to the high-water mark he's set for himself.

I ate a hearty meal. Then in came my kind host again, this time with a couple of rugs and pillows, which he put down on the sofa.

"And now, Jacques," he said, "I will wish you goodnight. I will lock you in and take away the key so that you may have your sleep and that no one may disturb you. But before I go, *mon brave garçon*, let me thank you for the inestimable service which you have rendered to me this night. Now, once more, *bonne nuit—à demain!*"

Then Monsieur Delmaine left me, and I was glad to hear the door locked, as it gave me such a safe feeling.

With a heart full of thankfulness to the God who had prospered me so far and protected me in peril, I lay down on the couchette, and in a few minutes was sound asleep and dreaming—dreaming—not as you'd suppose about the strange things that had just happened to me, but about the little gal who stole away my heart when I was a youngster, and, for all I knew, might have it still.

It is not often I remember dreams, but this one was so clear that it was like a picture, and I shall never forget it as long as I can call to mind anything at all.

It seemed to me that I was standing before a great black mountain, and all of a sudden a door opened in it. A tall figure, wrapped in a long cloak, stood just inside the doorway. The figure lifted one hand and beckoned to me, and though I didn't want to go and was trembling at the very idea, it seemed as if something was drawing me nearer and nearer, as I've heard said the snake draws the poor bird. On I went—fearing, unwilling, but still on—step by step, till I was there alone in the dark. Then a sort of hopeless feeling came over me, and I gave myself over for lost, when, all in a minute, I saw a bright light. Right in the middle of it, a young lass was standing with the lovely innocent face I remembered, only grown older and more beautiful—and the dark curls I used to think so pretty, quite long now, hung down her back. And I thought I stretched out my arms to her and cried, "Gabrielle, my child, is it thou?"

And the low sweet voice I loved answered, *"Yes, Jacques, it is thy little Gabrielle, and I have come to save thee."*

Then it seemed as if she laid those little hands of hers in mine, and together we stepped forward. The solid rock split before us, and we were out and standing in the sunlight. Then Gabrielle turned her face to me with such a strange, solemn look, and she pointed to the split rock. She said, *"See what love can do!"*

Then in a moment she was gone.

Maybe the dream repeated itself again and again. Anyway, I seemed to be dreaming it for hours, and it was with the words "See what love can do!" ringing in my ears that I waked at last.

"*Bonjour*, Jacques Hamon; are you rested?" said my host's kind voice through the door. "Good; then when you are ready, come into the next room and have some coffee."

After breakfast he took me back into the study and said, as he motioned me to sit down, "Now, Jacques, tell me all about your adventures yesterday."

So I began at the very beginning and went through it all, forgetting nothing. When I told him how I'd swum ashore and landed without being seen, he clapped me on the back and said, "*Bravo, mon brave garçon!*" And then at that point of the story where Monsieur Paul had passed me so close, and afterward, too, when I was dodging behind the boulder and listening to the talk of the three beauties in the cave—Monsieur Eustache Delmaine seemed to be almost holding his breath, he was so moved.

"Yes," he said, when I had finished, "you were quite right. Maître

Paul is Monsieur de St Rémy, and if he had seen you, he would
at once have guessed your errand, would have robbed you of the
packet you were carrying, and would certainly have found some
reason for depriving you of your liberty, if not of your life. For, of
course, it would be dangerous, he would argue, for a man to be at
large who could bear testimony against him being an eye-witness
to his robbery of the document that had been entrusted to you and
also to his taking part in the smuggling."

"But now, Monsieur," I said, "thank God, the danger is over."

"So far as the safety of the will is concerned, yes," replied my
host. "But the danger to yourself will not be over until you are back
on Sir Philip's yacht."

"But what good could it be to Maître Paul," I said, "to catch
me now?"

"Not much, certainly, but out of revenge he would do anything.
And, therefore, Jacques Hamon, you must act with the same caution
and discretion on your return journey as you showed coming here. I
wish I could wait till evening and help you, but I must start for Paris
at once; not a moment must be lost in getting the will into court.
My wife will see that you have all you require here during the day,
and when the night comes, you will find your way down the cliff
and give the signal from the pulpit—that is the name the ledge goes
by here. I trust you will get safely away to the yacht. Later, when I
return from Paris, I hope to send you a present to remind you that
Eustache Delmaine is not ungrateful for the great service you have
rendered to him and his."

"One thing more, Monsieur," I said. "Will Monsieur have the
goodness to give me a receipt for the packet I brought? A few
lines, just to show the Marquis and my master that I did my errand
faithfully?"

"With pleasure, Jacques," said Monsieur, and he went to his
writing table and scribbled a sentence or two on a sheet of paper,
put it in a wrapper, then sealed and addressed it to the Marquis de
Quedrennes. Then he bid me goodbye, telling me to count upon
him as a friend always. A carriage was waiting for him, and in a few
minutes he was off on his way to Paris.

My day passed pleasantly enough. Madame Delmaine was nearly as charming as her husband, and it really seemed as if she couldn't do enough for me. I felt quite ashamed, not being used to being made a fuss over, and was almost glad when evening came and the darkness settled down. I felt it was time to set out on my way back to the yacht.

"How glad my master and the Marquis will be to see me safe and my work done!" I said to myself as I got out into the copse once more and crept along towards the edge of the cliff where the zigzag path began. "And how proud I'll be to show my receipt and to hear Sir Philip say, 'I knew you'd do it, Jack, my boy! I never doubted you!'"

My heart was so light that I felt like singing as I walked on towards the rocky pathway leading to the pulpit. Still, I went through the copse as quietly as I could for prudence's sake, remembering my promise of my master. My tinder box was in my pocket. On reaching the ledge, I had nothing to do but light my flare. Before I set a light to it, however, I looked around everywhere, and I listened too, with all my ears, but there was nothing to be seen, nor yet to be heard. The place seemed quite lonely and quiet. Then I lighted my flare and let it burn for a second or two before stamping it out. And my heart just leaped for joy when, out in the offing, a rocket went hissing up into the sky, and I knew my signal was seen and answered, and the boat would put off for me at once. All was still—still as death—as I stepped out from the pulpit, took one last look all around and about me, and went down the cliff to the shore. The tide was coming up, but there was a good bit of beach still, and the dark mouth of the cave seemed quite a long way from the water.

I knew it must be some little time before the *Swift's* boat could reach the shore, so I made for my friend the big boulder, meaning to hide by it while I was waiting. Here once more, I turned to see if all was safe. But before I'd had time to get my face seaward again to look for the boat that was to fetch me away, there was a rush behind me from the cave—some muttered curses in French, and I felt my arms pinioned, while something very thick and woolly and stifling was thrown over my face and made fast behind. Then I felt a man on each side gripping me firm, and they began—though I resisted all I knew how—to hurry me up the cliff. I could see nothing with that wrapper over my face, and I kept stumbling over the stones. The men that led me yelled at me every time. I tried to call out, hoping that maybe my mates in the boat might hear me, but I was so choked with the muffler that I couldn't make a sound.

As we reached the top of the cliff, the cold, hard, bell-like voice that I knew and hated said just behind us—showing whose work it was that I was trapped like this—"To my house, my men! This must be the English government spy I have been watching for. I will take charge of him for one night, and tomorrow he shall be lodged in the fort prison. You have done well, my trusty coast guards, and you shall find it to your advantage."

Still pinioned and blindfolded, I was hurried along by the two men through the copse. Then the ground changed, and I could tell we had reached the clearing where Maître Paul's house was. I heard a door open with a key. The men said, "*Bonsoir, Monsieur le Capitaine,*" and a hand pushed me across the threshold and into a room. Then the hand drew the muffler from my head, and I found myself face to face with the wickedest-looking man I ever clapped eyes on. I've been around the world a good bit, and I've learned to know a good man when I see him, and a bad man, too, but Maître Paul's face was a lot worse than the worst I'd come across, except his own years ago. For I was right about that voice—I mean it was the same voice I'd heard that night at Jersey—and the face that was now before me was the same face (only grown older and wickeder) that I'd seen then. And the voice and the face were both the property of Monsieur Eustache Delmaine's enemy and rival, old Monsieur Pierre's disinherited nephew, Maître Paul de St Rémy.

Chapter Four

An Enemy Hath Done This

My hands were fast bound behind me, or I know I couldn't but have fallen upon that rascal and won my liberty in spite of him. But since I was helpless, there was nothing I could do but keep a bold front and wait for what might come.

The man would have been handsome except his eyes were too near together. Now, as they looked at me, they half shut and narrowed themselves till there was only just room to see that wicked soul of his peering out of its windows.

"*Eh bien!*" he said. "You're fairly caught now! Give an account of yourself. I do not know who you are, but *n'importe*—I know your errand—unless I am greatly mistaken. And first of all—your name."

His manner was so insulting, his words so short and rude (as if I was the very scum of the earth and nearly beneath his notice), that I felt my blood boil.

"Oh, for free hands! Oh, for a pair of strong *sabots* that would stand hard work!" I said to myself. But to him I said nothing. If I couldn't thrash and kick the scoundrel, as I was dying to do, at least I could vex and baffle him by keeping silence.

"Now then, you," he said. "Answer me! Your name?"

I smiled as carelessly and provokingly as I could in the scoundrel's face, but I never said a word.

"Ah, you think you can deceive me and that if you say nothing I shall know nothing," said Maître Paul. Then his blustering voice

changed to a friendly coaxing tone. "I advise you, *mon ami*," he
said with a smile far wickeder than his frown, "I advise you to
reconsider your position. Now," he smiled broader and showed
two sharp, tearing teeth, like a dog's, "if you were open and frank,
you understand, you would find me ready to meet you. Name your
terms for all the information you can give me, and for my part, I
promise I will be no miser."

To think I was like himself—to be bribed! But I only held my
head higher, looked full in his face, and laughed with contempt.

Monsieur de St Rémy's face changed all in a minute. He eyed me
as though he'd murder me if he dared. But behind that murderous
scowl of his was the shrinking of the coward that's ever the reverse
side of a bully. All his bravery and bluster came of my having my
hands tied. I knew that well enough, he could see I did, and he
ground his teeth over it. Then he came nearer to me and began to
search my pockets. He hadn't a notion—I could tell that by his eager
manner—that I'd been to Monsieur Delmaine and given up the
parchment. That was what he was hoping to find on me now.

His hands were trembling so that he could hardly get into
my vest pocket, and when at last he felt a paper there, he gave an
exclamation so fierce and triumphant that I wondered if something
wouldn't happen to him there and then, when he found out what
this paper really was.

Well, he drew it out of the pocket, held it close to the lamp,
and started as he saw the direction; a look of doubt and fear
came over his face, for of course it was addressed to the Marquis
de Quedrennes. With one wolfish glare at me, he tore open the
wrapper and saw written the form of receipt Monsieur Eustache
made out for me to show to them who had sent me on my errand.

As long as I live I shall never forget the howl of rage and despair
the scoundrel gave. No wild beast that I ever heard could begin to
come up to it. He dashed the paper down on the floor and turned to
me with his hands clenched.

"Is it indeed so?" he hissed, nearly choking with his fury. "Did
you deliver a parchment to Monsieur Eustache Delmaine?"

I said nothing, and he just wriggled and writhed like a worm on a fish hook.

"Will nothing make you speak?" he cried. "Tell me, at least, when you delivered the packet."

But I only smiled at him and held my peace. He swore at me— cursed me again and yet again. Then feeling, I suppose, that it was of no use trying to get anything out of me, he held open the door and motioned me to follow him. I did so, and he opened another door, and when I entered this room, which was dark, he went out and turned the key after him. In three minutes more I heard him giving some orders to a manservant, and then he slammed the front door with an angry bang. Just as well as if he'd told me, I knew he'd gone off to the château to find out if Monsieur Eustache had started for Paris yet or was still at home.

"Ah, Monsieur Eustache Delmaine," I said, "you knew the man you had to deal with when you set off for Paris this morning!" And, bound and a prisoner as I was, I couldn't forbear a chuckle to think how nicely we'd cheated this rascal.

But the rascal was back again in a quarter of an hour, and I heard him stamping and swearing about the place like a madman. He'd found out that Monsieur Eustache had given him the slip and concluded that the will was well on its way to be proven.

It was while Maître Paul was walking to and fro, stamping and muttering in the next room to me, that I heard a knock—very soft and low—at the front door. He opened it himself. Then I heard a heavy shuffling step following his into the room, and the door shut.

The deep, gruff voice I'd heard in the cave the night before said, "Maître Paul, what you gave Jean and me was only on account, you know, and now, as we are starting for Jersey tomorrow, I must ask you to have the goodness to pay us the rest—our share of the value of the goods we put away in your barn."

"And pray, how can I tell what they may be worth?" said Monsieur de St Rémy, speaking harshly and hastily. "It may be a parcel of rubbish you have brought me; it may be something perhaps impossible to dispose of. Why should I give you, beforehand, money which I may never get back?"

"Does Maître Paul, then, need to be reminded of our agreement?" said Simon. "Is it possible that Monsieur—?"

"Agreement, indeed!" interrupted Monsieur de St Rémy. "And do you really suppose that an agreement such as this, made between me and you two—Simon and Jean—can really bind me? Say another word about agreements, and I will throw up the whole business, and then where will you be? For neither of you has head enough to organize the thing. Now go! I have no more time to waste upon such *canaille* as you."

Simon muttered something under his breath which I couldn't hear, but the tone of his voice was threatening. If I'd been Maître Paul, I'd have tried to make friends with him before he went. But Maître Paul was full of the loss of that will, and he'd no patience to think or speak of anything else. He didn't come close to me any more that night, and after a while, though my hands and arms ached with being tied back so tight, I fell asleep for a few minutes at a time, after, in groping around, I'd found myself a chair to sit on. But I was glad to see the dawn creeping through the chinks of the window shutters, for the night had been a long one, and I was very weary and in pain, and hungry too. But Monsieur de St Rémy was not one of those who obey the command, "If thine enemy hunger, feed him; if he thirst, give him drink." And when the coast guard men came around for their orders about ten (as I guessed by the sun), I'd had nothing to eat or drink.

One of the men, when he and his mate came into the room where I was, seeing my hands and arms so swollen and bruised, said to Maître Paul, "Monsieur le Capitaine, with your permission, these cords should be taken off. *Le pauvre garçon* has suffered more than enough."

"*Non, non!*" Monsieur de St Rémy answered. If ever I saw a coward's fear in any face, I saw it in his then. "*Non, non!*" he said again. "Not until he is safely lodged in the fort cell."

The men took me between them as they'd done last night, only this time my face wasn't covered. We walked across the clearing, through a gate, and out onto the cliff, keeping as straight as we could go for about a mile till we came to a sort of promontory—a spur of the cliff jutting out over the sea. High up on this cape, and built of solid stone laid deep in the foundation of rock, was a small fort. It looked old and was weather-beaten like an old salt's face. The wall was thick, the windows barred, and in many places the walls and battlements were pierced with loops for arrow-shooting. Three or four cannons were mounted upon the wall facing the sea, but it wasn't likely they'd ever be much good, for no enemy would think of attacking a place like this, so lonely and out of the way and where there wasn't either glory or plunder to be had.

On the front of the spur of rock, the sea beat constant, and it came rolling in, too, but quieter, on the shingle beach to the left. But on the right side of the promontory, there was a sort of creek running up through a rock channel. At high tide, I should say, the creek would be full of water, but even at the ebb, it hadn't ought ever to be dry. The place was encircled with sea on all sides, save at the back, where the spur joined onto the cliff.

A little way out to sea, almost opposite the entrance to the narrow creek, stood a bare, desolate-looking little island, such as there's many of all along that coast. The lower rocks of it were flattish and seemed to be grown over with seaweed, or maybe shellfish, but the upper part was naked and brown. The whole lookout of cape and fort and island and wild sullen sea struck a sort of chill to my heart.

"There'll be no getting out of that," I said to myself as I looked at the thick walls of the fort rising out of the rock. "No getting out of that once you're in."

Maybe there was something of my thoughts in my face, for Maître Paul, who was walking near, turned his head every now and again to look at me and gave a wicked little laugh that showed his dog's teeth. He said, "Yes, this is a fine place for spies and traitors. *Vive l'Empereur*, and down with his enemies!"

I knew well enough that the first part of his speech was said to vex me, and the last was to make the coast guards think how loyal to the reigning government was their Captain. But the words and the hard laugh, more especial as I heard them in such pain of body and mind and on an empty stomach, made me feel as if I wasn't myself—the old Jacques—anymore, but only a poor, crushed, helpless, God-forsaken prisoner with dead walls closing in on him with no sort of hope for the future.

There seemed to be a little company of soldiers kept at the fort, some of the National Guard—those who were left behind when Napoleon took his pick for the army. There didn't seem to be any officer of rank in charge of the place, but we were received by an old sergeant, who must have seen active service—he was so scarred and cut about. This sergeant appeared to be head jailor, too; Monsieur Valdac, Maître Paul called him. He was a stout man with a good, honest face and a big military moustache. He looked at me close and keen as we entered the great bare waiting hall, where there was no furniture save a chair or two, an old table with a large book, an inkhorn, and some quill pens.

"Have you a warrant for this man's arrest, Monsieur de St Rémy?" inquired Monsieur Valdac.

"No, it was needless," said Maître Paul. "He was caught red-handed."

"Doing what?" asked the sergeant.

"Spying, sneaking about. He is English and has friends among the military and naval authorities to whom he sells all the information he can obtain."

"And his name, Monsieur le Capitaine?"

"Oh! Yes—his name. I did know, but I have forgotten," said Maître Paul.

Monsieur Valdac looked up at him from his seat at the table, where he had the big book before him and into which he was entering the particulars given him. It was a curious look, I thought; there was distrust in it, and dislike too, and my heart warmed to the old fellow then and there.

The sergeant turned to me and said gently and nicely, "Your name, if you please, *mon garçon*?"

"Jacques Hamon, Monsieur," I said.

"And you are an Englishman, as Monsieur de St Rémy signifies?"

"*Non*, Monsieur, not by birth. I come from the island of Jersey, but I have lived in England many years."

"And what is your occupation, Jacques Hamon?"

"Did I not tell you, Valdac?" said Maître Paul. "What use in questioning this fellow? A spy is nothing if he be not a liar."

The old soldier said nothing to this interruption but repeated quietly, not raising his voice, "Your occupation, Jacques Hamon?"

"Sailor on board the yacht *Swift*, belonging to Sir Philip Penreath, English baronet," I said.

"Then where does the spy come in?"

"He does not come in at all, Monsieur," I said. "It is a false accusation. But the truth is, I am dangerous, and so—"

The old sergeant stopped me with a look; it was a look that said a great deal and gave me courage to believe things would come right yet.

"The miscreant! How dare he?" cried Maître Paul, raising a stick in a threatening way over my head.

"Monsieur de St Rémy," said the old man, his face flushed with anger, "you forget yourself. You have no right to threaten my prisoners. As to Jacques Hamon, am I to understand that you assume the whole responsibility of his detention here? If so, you must please say so in writing, that I may have it to show in case inquiry be made."

Not over and above willing, Monsieur de St Rémy did as he was asked. Then, looking daggers at the old man and me, he turned and stalked out of the fort, and the air seemed somehow easier to breathe when he was gone.

"Jacques Hamon," said the sergeant, turning to me again, "this young soldier, Charlais, will take you to your cell. No. 1, Charlais, where the old man lately lodged, and see that the prisoner's hands and arms are bathed and rubbed with oil. Also, get him some food. You look as if you had not broken your fast today, *mon pauvre garçon*," said he, with his keen, kind eyes on my face.

"It is so, Monsieur," I said. "I have had no food since my supper last night at the house of Monsieur Eustache Delmaine."

"Ah, so you had business with him! A most worthy gentleman, and much respected here," said Monsieur Valdac. "But, enough for the present! Take him away, Charlais; see that my instructions are carried out, and forget not to search the prisoner."

I followed the young soldier, Charlais, who led me out into a corridor and up some stone steps, onto a broadish landing, and out of it four doors opened. The first on the right he unlocked, and I followed him in. This part, anyone might know at a glance, wasn't made for a prison, but had only lately, during the war-time, been used for the safekeeping of the few prisoners that were taken up here and there.

The cell was not a bad sort of room, save that it was rather bare. It had whitewashed stone walls and a good-sized window looking over onto the creek. It was barred outside but was set low enough in the wall to see out of, even when you were sitting down.

A narrow iron bedstead in the back part of the cell, a chair, a table, a wooden box for prisoners' clothes, and a few nails in the wall for hanging such as couldn't be put away folded—these, and a straw mat by the bedside, were all the furniture.

"This is your room," said Charlais. "Now I will go and fetch warm water and oil, but first I will cut those cords." And he produced a knife from his pocket.

"Ah!" he cried out as he cut the cords. My hands dropped, powerless. "But you have been cruelly bound! *Pauvre garçon!* Either you must be very bad or you were wrongly judged." And he looked me in the face close and curious, as if to see which was the truth.

Then he went away, and I sat down on the box and looked about me. Scarce had my eyes gone well around the room, when I started to my feet with a cry, being altogether surprised and delighted, for there, on the white wall, right opposite the window, where the light fell full upon it, was sketched in charcoal, the face and figure of a young maid. It was done so skillfully that it seemed to stand out against the white background almost as if it had life. But the face— ah, the face was the one I'd loved as a boy, the face that had come to me in my dream. And once again, as in the dream, my lonely, aching heart cried out for her, and I said, "Ah, my little Gabrielle, is it thou?"

And though I knew it was only a picture and couldn't answer, such comfort came to me—to say nothing of the wonder as to how the drawing got there—from this charcoal sketch. When I was able to take my eyes from that picture, I saw that in other places, too, there were drawings. Some were lifelike while others were some of the most fanciful ideas that I ever set eyes on.

When Charlais came back with a jug of hot water, a little oil, and some rags, plus half a loaf, a piece of cheese, and a mug of cider, I said to him, "Please tell me how all these drawings came to be on the wall. So far as I can judge, they seem to be very well done."

"*Holà oui!*" said Charlais. "They are the work of a prisoner who had this cell till quite lately, but we were obliged to move him next door, for he was found at his window signaling to someone outside. As we had a very strict man then in the place Monsieur Valdac now has, the old artist was moved to the cell on that side." And Charlais touched the wall against which the head of my bed stood. "For that one," Charlais went on, "has the land view, and there the sentry paces up and down night and day."

"Then the old man is an artist?" I said, as Charlais set to work doctoring me.

"No," replied the young soldier, tearing up a rag and soaking it in oil. "I only call him so out of compliment. He was a journalist, I believe, and was put in here for writing against the Emperor."

"And how long has he been in this place?" I asked.

"About a year," said Charlais. "But I must not talk so much, or Monsieur Valdac will be calling me to order. He says I am a gossip, and perhaps it is true. It is so dull living in this place, and when I find anyone new to talk to, my tongue goes too fast. But now I will say *au revoir* for the present. Do you feel any better, *mon pauvre garçon?*"

"Yes, indeed, thanks to your kindness, Charlais," I said.

Then the young chap smiled, nodded, and went away. When I'd eaten my dinner, I lay down on the bed to rest. I didn't feel lonely either, at least not so much as you'd think, considering it was my first day in prison. But gradually I found my thoughts getting mixed, and before long I fell asleep and didn't wake up once till my supper came at eight in the evening.

Chapter Five

On the Other Side of the Wall

Sleeping half the day, as I'd been doing, wasn't very good for my night's rest, and long after all the lights were out and the whole place quiet, I was lying wide awake, staring into the darkness and thinking of all that had happened to me since I left the yacht. At least it was a comfort to me that before I was caught by Maître Paul and his men, I had time to show my flare. As that was the signal we agreed upon to show that the will was in safekeeping, Sir Philip and the Marquis would be easy in their minds as to that, though I knew my dear master would be fretting at my not getting back to him. He would understand well enough who had got me arrested, for that was the danger he warned me against, but he did not know where I was hidden away, so he could not send help to me. I wondered what he would do. It wouldn't be safe for him to keep on cruising about in French waters for very long, and yet he'd feel as if he ought not to give up trying to find out something about me.

Then my thoughts took a new turn, and I began to think of Gabrielle, wishing it were light so that I could see the picture on the wall, if only for company. But, all of a sudden, I remembered that in the pocket of my breeches was the tinder-box with flint and steel, and likewise a candle-end Madame Delmaine gave me in case I wanted a light when I was hid anywhere. Charlais had searched me after a fashion, and he took away my knife, but he left me the tinder-box, saying there was no harm in that. So up I got and felt about in the dark for the breeches that were hanging up on a nail. Yes—here they were, and in a minute I found my box. But, unhappily, as I was hanging the breeches up again, the box slipped out of my hand and went rattling and clanging down on the stone floor, making such a noise in the place that I thought I should have the jailors up in a minute or two. But the minutes went by and nobody came, so I made up my mind that the folks slept sound at the fort, and glad enough I was to know it, since it might prove useful sometime.

I struck a light, and my candle was burning up clear and bright as I stood in front of the charcoal picture, when I heard, just by the head of my bed, a gentle tapping on the wall.

"That must be the old man, and I've woken him with my racket," I said to myself. And, not to seem unsociable, I took up my box and struck on the wall with the corner of it.

Then the rapping on his side began again, but not like the first three or four regular knocks; now it was one—then a stop, then on it would go for several more, then stop again, till I thought the prisoner must be mad and just amusing himself this odd way.

All of a sudden I remembered hearing of a kind of language folks had made (just by tapping) so that they could talk to each other without saying a single word. It was a precious slow language and uncertain at best, for you had to keep saying the alphabet over all the time like infants in a dame's school, the number of raps deciding the letters forming the word. For instance, one rap would stand for A, two for B, and so on. But it would need a deal of practice before one could do it quick. However, it seemed to me as if this was maybe what the old man was trying to do. So then I began to spell out the raps, but he being, as I suppose, in the middle of a sentence, I could make nothing of it till he came to a stop and then began again. By this time I made out three words, and those three were French for the question "Who are you?" and I answered very slowly (for it was difficult talking that way), "A sailor from England."

"Why are you here?" rapped out the man.

"Accused of spying," I answered, but I can't be sure I spelled it right, having gotten a bit mixed up in my alphabet and French spelling.

"Accused of what?" came the question—showing I had not made things clear.

"Spying," I rapped.

"Your accuser?" asked the old prisoner.

"Monsieur Paul de St Rémy."

And as soon as I gave this answer, I heard him, all of sudden, scrape and scratch hard on the wall with the tool he'd been tapping with, as if the sound of the man's name angered him, and he could show his anger no other way. Presently he rapped out, "Traitor! Thief! Spy!"

Then it was my turn to scrape hard on the wall and rap out "Smuggler," to end up with—and a nice list of honorable professions they made.

The old fellow seemed to take some time digesting that last word of mine, but at last he tapped, "Have you found the cold chisel?"

"No," I answered. "What chisel?"

"Girl's shoe."

What could that mean? I was fairly puzzled for a minute, then it came on me like a flash. "I must look for it somewhere near that picture so like Gabrielle. That is the only girl there is here," I said to myself. So I took up my candle and went and stood in front of the charcoal sketch. The flickering light in the draughts from door and window made such a lot of changes in the face, causing smiles and dimples and moving of eyelids and what not, that I felt quite strange as I was looking at it, but an impatient tap from the other side of the wall made me begin to search for the tool in earnest.

"Girl's shoes?" I thought. Seeing nothing, I began to pass my hand over the wall about the feet of the drawing. As I did so, all of a sudden I felt something, and sure enough there was an old cold chisel stuck in between two stones, right up to within less than half an inch of the top and not showing the least bit in the world till you looked quite close, feeling it there.

I pulled it out and went back to my place by the bed and tapped "Found." But this time there was no answer, and while I was still listening for the old man to begin again, I heard steps up the stone stair to our landing. It was the night-warder making his round to see that the doors were closed and that all was safe.

I blew out my light and lay down on my bed in case he should come in, but he did not trouble to do that. And after a minute or two, I heard his heavy foot on the stair again, down, down, fainter and farther, till he was gone.

Then the old man rapped out, *"Au revoir—á demain!"* from which I suppose that he thought we had done enough talking for one night.

It was late now—after twelve—and I was getting sleepy again, so I went to bed and to sleep and knew nothing more till a loud bell, somewhere near, clanged so hard that I woke up dreaming that somehow I had got into a belfry and was nearly stunned with the noise of the Sunday morning ringing.

The big bell rang for us to get up, and when I was ready, I made my bed and swept the cell floor, Charlais having left a broom the night before, telling me what to do. There seemed to be no work for the prisoners, save the keeping of their cells clean and tidy. Of course, in a small place like this, there was no regular discipline, so prison life here was not what it usually is. And for me, that had always been used to plenty of work, it was dull and disheartening to dawdle about my little room with nothing to do but to look out of the window or at the pictures on the walls all day.

There was not a sound from my old neighbor on the other side of the wall, so I suppose he did not think it safe to begin a conversation in the daytime, when the soldiers were going about and Monsieur Valdac might be in at any moment.

It was just after my dinner of bread, soup, fried potatoes, and hard cider, and I was standing at the open window, looking out over the creek and the cliff beyond it, when the key of my door turned in the lock, and in walked the sergeant.

"Bonjour, Jacques Hamon," he said. "I come to have a little

conversation with you and find out, if I can, the nature of your offense and the true reason of your arrest by Monsieur de St Rémy."

"Will Monsieur Valdac have patience to listen to my story?" I asked.

"*Mais certainement, mon garçon*; is it not for this that I am now come?"

"Then, so far as I can, without betraying confidence, I will give an account of myself," I said. "And Monsieur le Sergent shall see for himself in what, if in anything, I am to blame."

The kind old soldier sat down on my one chair, and I sat on the box. Then I began and told him my story quite straightforward and plain, keeping back nothing save only the name of the Marquis and the nature of the parchment that I had been sent over to deliver to Monsieur Delmaine. All I said about the will was that it seemed a very precious paper, and Monsieur de St Rémy wanted, above all things, to get hold of it. When he found he had lost it, and through me (the receipt in my pocket telling him this), he was so furious with me that he was ready to do anything.

The old sergeant listened with his eyes as well as his ears, but when I got to my dodging behind the boulder to hear the talk in the cave, and how afterwards I had both seen and heard Maître Paul and found out for certain that he was hand and glove with the smugglers, a big scar across the old man's face turned red as fire, he was so greatly excited.

"Ha," he said, "*mon garçon*. This is what I have long suspected, but suspicion is not proof, *malheureusement*. But now, Jacques, if this story of yours be true—and upon my soul, I see no reason to doubt it—you will—"

But here the warm-hearted, imprudent old man seemed all of a sudden to call to mind that he was a jailor and I but a prisoner, and that he ought not to make too free. And he looked so distraught and uncomfortable that I went on as if continuing my story.

"And the hardest part of it, Monsieur le Sergent," I said, "is that I am so helpless. My friends in the yacht do not even know where I am, and I have no means of communication with them. So, how can I ever prove my innocence or be set free?"

"Yes, *mon pauvre* Jacques; it is indeed hard! There is nothing for you but to trust in the *bon Dieu*, who is here as everywhere, and who will not suffer the innocent to be oppressed unavenged, or the wicked to triumph always. For the rest, Jacques, you shall have such indulgence as my duty permits me to give you. I wish I could do more to comfort you, *mon enfant*."

"I thank you, my kind jailor. Your words of sympathy help me much. I will trust in God, as you say, and somehow—perhaps—He will make for me a way of escape."

"Of escape, Jacques Hamon? Mean you of escape from the fort—from prison?"

"Who knows, Monsieur le Sergent?" I said. "Such things have happened before; they may again."

"Nay, *mon garçon*; dream not of that," said Monsieur Valdac. "If you tried to get away from this place, you would only lose your life, or be caught again and brought back, and then I should have to be much more strict with you."

"All I said, Monsieur," I answered, "was that maybe the good God, if I trusted in Him, would make a way of escape for me. And if He did make it, Monsieur Valdac, and put it before me, I should most certainly avail myself of it. It is but fair to tell you this."

The old sergeant knew not what answer to make to that. I could see he was hoping that God would help me in some other way than escaping from prison while he was jailor. His kind, puzzled face was so droll that it almost made me laugh, downhearted though I felt. He rose from his seat and moved to the door now, having come to the end of what he had to say on the subject of Providence and the good of trusting.

"Charlais will attend to your wants," he said as he unlocked my door again. "And if you desire anything—in reason, of course—that he does not supply, ask me, and if I can, I will let you have it."

I thanked him once more. Then he went away, and I turned back to the window and looked across the creek again.

There had been no one in sight when I was gazing out before, but now, standing at the further edge of the split in the cliff that made the creek, was a young woman. She was dressed as a Breton peasant, in a short, dark skirt and black jacket, and a neat white cap and apron. Her face was toward the island when I saw her first, but in a minute more, she turned towards the fort and faced my window full. I could not make out her features well, but what I did see made my heart beat quick.

"Out upon you for a fool, Jack!" I said to myself. "You are so full of your fancies now that every goose is a swan, and every woman makes you think of Gabrielle and imagine a likeness."

Well, the maid stood there looking over at my window for quite a long while. Then the hand she was shading her eyes with dropped to her side, her head hung down, and she turned and walked away towards the little village lying about half a mile inland. I could see her lift her apron and wipe her eyes as though she were crying.

Poor little soul! She was heavy-hearted about something. It seemed to me that she looked disappointed when she glanced up at my window, just as if she had missed seeing someone she was used to.

"Ah! I have it!" I said to myself. "Charlais said that the old man had this room till just now, and maybe she was accustomed to finding him at the window at a certain time in the day and is grieving not to see him now. Who knows! She may be his daughter, or niece, or something. I wish I could have seen her a bit nearer!" I turned away from the window and faced the pretty, sweet picture on the wall. "I wish I could, if only to see if she is really like this. Ah, well, I must have another talk with my old friend tonight, and maybe he will tell me his story and who this charcoal maid may be that stands out so lifelike on my wall."

The day seemed endless. The afternoon dragged as if it had been a week. But at last came supper-time, and after that the fort gradually settled down into quiet, and nothing could be heard but the splash of the sea against the cliff.

Before the lights were put out, I took the cold chisel from its hiding place in the wall, where it had formed a bit of the heel in the maid's shoe.

"Now," I thought, "if the old man asks me about it again, I can say I have it handy."

It seemed strange sitting there alone in the dark, waiting for that soft tapping on the wall. I was not by nature subject to odd notions or out-of-the-way feelings, but I could hardly say I was quite comfortable. I gave a gasp of relief and felt hot all over for a minute at the joy of realizing someone near when the first gentle rap sounded on the wall. I answered by another, and then my neighbor tapped the sentence:

"*Bonsoir, mon ami!* Have you got the cold chisel?"

"It is here," I replied.

"Then move your bed-head aside and look for a loose stone in the wall."

I moved the bed, went down on my knees, and feeling about in the darkness (for my candle-end was burnt out), I presently found a place in the wall where some bits of mortar had fallen out, and a large stone was loose. I laid hold of the stone by a corner that was sticking out and worked it backwards and forwards with both hands, prying out more mortar now and again with the chisel. And at last, after about half an hour's work, I managed, without noise too, to get the stone right out, leaving a hole about as big as my head; for happily this was only a partition wall, one stone thick, put up perhaps during the last year or two when some of the rooms of the fort had to be turned into cells.

I set the piece of rough stone down softly on the floor, and as I did so, I heard a deep sob. Then a cold, thin, trembling hand came through the hole, and mine went to meet it, and we two poor lonely prisoners grasped hands. The old prisoner whispered, "God bless you! I think I can bear it now."

And the young prisoner, his own voice sounding a bit shaky, and his eyes wet, answered:

"Thanks to God, so can I."

Chapter Six

The Story of Antoine Claireau

Our hearts were too full to say much at first, neither of us having much voice. But after a while the old man said:

"Put away the chisel in its old place; carefully, mind—it is a precious thing, and we could not replace it if lost. You will wonder how I, a prisoner, ever came to have such a tool here. It was this way. When I occupied the cell you have now, the stonework round the window had broken away, and the bars were thought to be insecure. So a workman was sent to do the needful repairs, and when he left the prison after finishing his job of work, he never noticed that his chisel had slipped over the edge of his tool bag and gotten into a dark corner; but I soon spied it out, and for safety's sake hid it in the wall where you found it. I should have taken it with me when I moved, but the jailor gave me only the shortest notice, and I was not left alone for a minute."

"And what did you do your tapping with?" I asked.

"I pulled out one of the hanging nails from the wall here and used that," said the old man. "But there is no need for rapping now; we can converse without hindrance. Only, *mon garçon*, ere you lie down to rest, you must be careful to put back the stone so as not to attract attention should anyone move the bed. Also, you had better sweep up the bits of mortar and throw them out of your window. We must take the utmost care not to excite suspicion, or we shall never make our escape."

"Make our escape?" I said. "Do you imagine such a thing possible?"

"I know not," he answered, "but this I know, that but for the hope of escape I should have died or gone mad during the first month of my imprisonment."

"Then you mean to try?" I said.

"*Mais certainement!*" he said, and there was that in his voice that showed me he had made up his mind to get away, even if his breaking out of prison should cost him his life.

"The one thing I have had all my life till now, Jacques Hamon," he said, "the one thing I have clung to when I have lacked nearly all else has been my liberty of action and of thought—liberty to believe, to speak, to write as I pleased. And from this love of mine—the love of liberty—have sprung many of my troubles. I should like to tell you something of my history, unless, perhaps, I should weary you."

"*Au contraire, mon camarade*," I said. "I am very much interested. Indeed, in such a life as ours here, your companionship and any confidence you may give me will be a real help, for thus I shall, for a season, forget my own troubles."

"Thanks, friend Jacques," said the old man. "My story, right from the commencement, would be too tedious for you to hear as for me to tell. Enough if I gave you just a brief sketch of my life with its many trials. My name is Antoine Claireau. My parents died of a pestilence when I was but a youth, so that I was early thrown upon my own resources. When I was a lad of sixteen, I entered a printer's office and remained there until I was twenty. It was here that I learned to love reading and determined that someday I, too, would write what others might read. My master was a poor-spirited fellow and never dared to print what the government might not like, so all he could venture to issue was some almanac or book of devotion. But he used to fill up his almanacs with short passages taken from books or journals, and after a time he turned over the task of selecting these passages to me. Well, Jacques, you may guess that from copying the extracts, I came to editing and altering them, and from editing to writing them out of my own head. So it was that I first became an author! But at last, by some accident, the printer found out that his foreman (for I had risen to this place) was also a writer. He was one of those old-fashioned people who

had a prejudice against men educating themselves beyond what
he considered their station, and because he himself was a spiritless
plodder, content never to advance a step, and quite without all
ambition, laid down the same law for everybody.

"'Antoine Claireau,' he said to me, the day after he had made
the discovery of my crime, for crime it was in his eyes, 'Antoine
Claireau, I am not a genius myself, and—'

"I was conceited and saucy enough in those days, and I
interrupted my master with—

"'It is true, Monsieur.'

"'What I was going to say, Antoine,' said the printer, turning
very red and angry, 'was that being no genius myself, but devoted
only and wholly to my trade, I had made up my mind to keep no
genius in my employ, taking up in writing the time that he owed to
me and using my machines for printing his own rubbish.'

"I might have told him, Jacques, and told him truly, that I
composed the 'rubbish' in my own time, and that at any rate, his
almanacs had sold far better since I began to write in them myself
instead of using the snippings of other men's work. But I was too
proud and too indignant to say a word in self-defense. I merely
replied, '*Très bien, monsieur*; when shall I leave you?'

"And when he said, 'At the end of the week,' I responded once
more, 'Very well, monsieur,' and we had no more conversation about
that matter.

"So, on the Saturday following, I took my wages and my bag of
clothes, left the printing office, and I never saw the printer again.

"From that time, for about ten years, my life was one of
continual change. I wrote for a newspaper—but this was seldom,
for we had hardly any journals then—then I did hack work for
booksellers, and then I set to my old work of printing for a time.
Next came a long illness, when I was taken to the hospital, and
where the devotion of a young sister of mercy, a nurse in our ward,
was the means of saving my life.

"When at last I recovered and left the hospital, I carried with
me the promise of Marcelline Prideaux that, as soon as I found
work and could make a home for her, she would be my wife. In six

months we were married. By that time I was already thirty-five years of age, and having proved to my cost the uncertainty of an author's life, I determined to stick to the printers' trade. For a while I went as foreman to a man in good business, and then at last, when he wished to retire, I took the whole affair off his hands upon terms advantageous to us both.

"The next ten years were the happiest of my life. My wife proved to be a treasure. My little daughter, Rielle—our only child— was the joy and sunshine of a home where only peace and harmony were to be found. But at last came a terrible change. A neighbor of ours, a dear lady, fell ill of typhus fever, and my Marcelline, with whom nursing had always been a passion, tended her night and day until she was convalescent. But the price of that recovery was the ruin of my life. My poor wife, wearied by the long strain upon her health, took the disorder and died in the crisis.

"I will not dwell upon that terrible time, when all hope seemed gone and I felt as though there was nothing left for me but to curse God and die. It was only my child's distress that roused me from mine. Her innocent helplessness, her dependence upon me, showed me what a wicked thing was my despair. Again I set to work with frantic energy, and the work saved me from madness or crime.

"So time passed on until my little one was about twelve years old. Then an old *bonne*, who had been with us from my marriage, died, and I could not trust a new servant to look after Rielle in such a place as Paris. So I sent her to Jersey, to my married sister, Madame Genette, who had offered to give her a home.

"Then came our great Revolution. Jacques, you say you are half English, and it is well for you that you are. Pray for your country, if you love it, that you may have no such time as we have known in France. And yet it was a noble time at its beginning. I saw when the first National Assembly stood up in the Versailles tennis court and swore to win their liberty. I helped—yes, even I—when we took the Bastille. I saw when the king—poor, good man—took the oath to keep the Constitution, and I remember how we all embraced, like brothers, and felt sure that our beautiful dreams were coming true at last. I was a member of the Great Jacobin Club. You have heard of that, Jacques Hamon?"

"I have heard no good of it," I said. "What I know is in a book that I have heard Sir Philip reading to the Marquis, a book by the great Mr. Burke, all about dens of murderers and the like."

"Ah, I know his name," said old Antoine, taking me up quick and sharp. "And a great man he was, as you say, but too ready to think evil of men who tried to do their duty. We had murderers among us, but we were not all villains. The best of us stood up for mercy and spoke against the butchery. Ah! What orators we had. But all was in vain. That cold-hearted pedant, Robespierre, conquered; my poor little journal was suppressed for daring to plead for justice, and I had to fly for my life and skulk in caves and woods through the time of the Terror. Jacques, *mon ami*, I cannot tell you of those months when I was hunted like a wild beast. Hardly a friend would dare to help me; every sound I thought was the murderers coming to seize me. I thanked God every day that my child was safe out of France. I thanked God that my wife was safe in heaven. For all France went mad with fear, and Robespierre and his gang were more afraid than all the rest, and that was what made them cruel."

"Very much as it is with my friend Maître Paul," I thought, but I said nothing.

"One thing, and one only, kept me from giving myself up to the guillotine," Antoine went on, after stopping a minute or so, "and that was the thought of my poor little Rielle. The child should not be left fatherless as well as motherless if I could help it. This gave me strength to live through those terrible days till Robespierre met the fate which he had brought upon so many wiser and better men than himself, and we thought that now, at least, we were free.

"I came back to Paris with my friends, the poor remnant of those who had loved justice and truth. We re-established our journals, we spoke in public, we hoped at last to be happy and united. Alas!" And through the hole in the wall, I could hear him sighing heavily like a man in a bad dream.

"And why should you not have been all right?" I asked, for I had often puzzled my brains over French politics, which seemed such a confusion to me that I never could make head nor tail of them. "Surely," I said, "you had made a clean enough sweep of all those old oppressions."

"*Ma foi, oui!*" he said, his voice so harsh and bitter that I could tell just how he was living those old times all over again. "We had pulled down the Bastille, leaving not a stone of it standing, but we had built nothing instead. And now a little Corsican came along and built a modern fortress in its place, ten times as strong. We had killed our poor King Log—Louis—and now we have a King Stork— Napoleon, as he calls himself. Yes, we are just the frogs in the fable all over again!"

It sounded odd even then to hear the old man talking of the French as frogs, which was just the nickname the English sailors always gave them in joke. Of course, Antoine didn't know that, and I was not going to tell him.

"I will not make too long a story, Jacques," the old man went on. "We overcame all our enemies, as you know, and our armies overran Italy, Switzerland, Holland, and Germany. But our soldiers conquered us as well as our enemies, and the best general was our lord and master. We would not see for a long time that we were under a stronger power than our kings ever exercised, but gradually we learned what we had done.

"I had gone on with my little journal. The *Cry of the Crowd* I called it, for it was the voice of those who had none other to speak for them. But I was careful never to say too much against the First Consul, as Bonaparte called himself then. One thing I had learned in my early printing days, and that was to write so that no one could take hold of my language and twist it into treason. But, one by one, all around me, I saw my old friends silenced, and my turn came at last."

"But surely they would not put you in prison merely for writing?" I said.

"Not for that only, Jacques," he answered in his bitter way. "Dear me, no. But I, if you please, I—the old Jacobin and Republican—was a Royalist conspirator, plotting to murder the great First Consul. That is why I am here."

"And how did they make that out?" I asked.

"I was still publishing my little paper," he continued, "and though the government checked its circulation all they could, there was no pretext for suppressing it. I had a few clever writers who shared my opinions and could still plead for liberty in moderate words. But one day I was applied to for work by a young man whom I had known in the Revolution time who called himself Robert Leroi. He had been of the Jacobin Club and had supported Robespierre till just before his fall."

"One moment, Antoine," I said. "Did he call himself Leroi through the Terror? From what I have heard, men have lost their heads for less than having a name like that."

"You are right, Jacques; he had taken some classical name, then. Citizen Cassius, I think it was, because he had not killed Caesar, I suppose. Well, Cassius or Leroi, or whatever his name was, was a clever fellow. I never liked him—he was too smooth and secret in his ways for my fancy—but he wrote well and had a gift for holding up the government to ridicule, and yet the police never troubled us on account of his articles, biting as they often were. Ah! Now I know why that was."

"You mean that he was one of those spies," I said. And, indeed, I was beginning to see a family likeness in this young man to someone I knew only too well. Nor had I forgotten either the angry scrape old Antoine had made on the wall when I rapped out Monsieur Paul de St Rémy's name that first night we had our tapping conversation.

"That is it, *mon ami*," he said. "And he was constantly goading me on to be bolder in my writing, pointing to his own articles and saying that the Government was afraid to meddle with us. I believed him—fool that I was! And at last, when the First Consul was to be made Emperor, I wrote a protest—foolish enough, though true—calling on the people to judge between the old Bourbon kings and the new ruler and see which was the harder master. That was the end. The article was twisted into evidence of a plot for the restoration of the Bourbons. I was arrested in the name of the Emperor, and my paper was suppressed. The police discovered, concealed in my office, Royalist proclamations, white ribbons, daggers, and I know not what else."

"And I can more than guess who put them there," I said.

"So can I, now," answered poor Antoine, very sadly. "But then, I never even suspected Robert Leroi till I learned from the magistrate who examined me that the young man was really a spy of the police."

"And how was it that you were sent here, of all places in the world?" I asked of my fellow prisoner.

"Ah! That, too, was my good friend Robert's doing," he said. "The police did not want to have a public trial, for fear of their dirty trickery being found out, so I was told that, by the singular clemency of the Emperor, I was to be imprisoned here for life. Through an old Republican friend, now in the police, I managed to send word to my daughter in Jersey, and she followed me hither. But I firmly believe I was sent to this place because Robert Leroi knew the neighborhood and wanted me to be under his own eye. He is often about here, I think. Once, when I was in your present quarters, I saw him on the cliff and asked Charlais if that were not the government spy, Robert Leroi."

"And he replied, of course, that he was nothing of the kind," I said.

"Yes," replied Antoine. "Charlais told me his real name and that he is the captain of the coast guards. It seems he lives not very far from here, in a house on the cliff, and if I remember rightly, Charlais called him Monsieur Paul de St Rémy."

"Then you and I, *mon ami*," I said, "have another bond of union, for the spy and traitor, the black-hearted, treacherous scoundrel that put you in here has done the same kind office for me, and if ever I get out—"

There was silence for a moment, and then the old man said—in a low voice, but firm and confident as if he was free already, "And when I do—"

Then neither of us said a word more, but through that hole in the wall, he once again put his hand and gripped mine. For all he was so old and worn, his grasp felt strong enough to stop Paul de St Rémy's lying breath, if the old man ever got a good hold on him.

Chapter Seven

Speeding the Parting Guest

"Thank you for your story, Antoine," I said when the old man got through. "You must have suffered greatly."

"Yes, Jacques, *vous avez raison*; I have indeed suffered. But now, *mon ami*, that you know something of my past life, let me also tell you a little about my plans for the future."

"But first, Antoine," I said, "may I ask you a question or two?"

"As many as you please, my friend," answered the old man.

"That little daughter of yours is no longer in Jersey?"

"No, Jacques, no," he said. "As soon as she learned that I had been removed from Paris here, she left her aunt at St Héliers and traveled to Brittany. She is not far from here now and is lodging in the village."

"And when she lived in Jersey, Antoine, did she bear your name of Claireau?"

"No," said the old fellow, "her aunt thought it safer and better that she should drop my name. So my poor little girl had to try and forget what her father called her—Rielle Claireau— and call herself Gabrielle Genette. However—but what ails you, *mon garçon*? Why clasp you thus my hand? What mean you by that fervent 'Thank God! Thank God!'?"

"Oh, *mon ami*!" I cried. "Then you are her father—hers? Ah, how happy I am—how very happy!"

"*Tiens*, Jacques Hamon, you surely must be going mad, my

son. What is there to make anyone happy in the fact that I am my daughter's father?"

"And you it was who drew the sketch of her here on my wall?"

"*Mais certainement*! I have been artist as well as journalist. But what of it? You know not the maiden."

"Pardon! I do know her, Antoine. I knew and loved her when she was a child in Jersey. I was but a youth, and she was still a little girl, but I so loved her that I have never had even a passing fancy for another, and I have always been hoping and longing to see her again."

There was silence on both sides of the wall for a minute or two, but at last old Antoine said, "*Bon!* Such constancy deserves reward. You are a good youth. Now show yourself as brave and determined as I judge you to be faithful and true. Let us together plan and effect our escape, and then—well then, ask what you will, and I shall not refuse you."

As the old man spoke, I felt, all of a sudden, as if there was nothing I couldn't do. For, somehow or other, confessing my love of Gabrielle to her father seemed to make me twice the man I'd ever been before.

"Antoine," I said, "we will escape! God will help us, and one day I shall say to you the words your little Rielle said to me in a dream only the other night. 'See,' she said, 'see what love can do!'"

"Now, listen to me, Jacques," said the old man. "My daughter lodges in the village with a baker's family. The baker's wife is the sister of our Charlais. Charlais goes there for the Sunday once a month, and being a good-hearted young man, he sometimes brings me a message from my child. For a time after I came here, it seemed as though it would be impossible to establish any communication with the outside world. But after a month or two, when I was in the cell you have now, seeing that Rielle always walked by the creek-side where she could get a good view of my window, I began to have a good hope of escaping someday. For I thought I could make her understand by signs what I required, and she would contrive somehow to let me have the things I wanted. But one day, when I was signaling to my child, the jailor who was here before Monsieur Valdac came in unexpectedly and caught me at it, and the next day I was moved in here."

"Then the girl I saw by the creek was Gabrielle," I said. "That accounts for her looking so disappointed and unhappy when she spied me at the window."

"Yes, she has far sight, my little Rielle, and the difference between your young head and my old one with its white hair, she could not fail to notice at once, even at that distance," said Antoine. "But now, Jacques, we must get her to help us; for without her, we can do nothing."

"*Eh bien, mon ami*; then what would you have me do?" I said.

"Watch for her again tomorrow, *mon fils*, and when you see her, show her this first of all." And the old man shoved through the gap in the wall what felt like a silk kerchief.

"It is a red scarf that she gave me herself," he said. "She bought it with the first money she ever earned, and I have kept it by me ever since. When she sees that, she will know that you are in my confidence and that we are working together."

"I see," I said. "And what then?"

"Then, Jacques, when you see you have my daughter's full attention, you must take hold of one of the iron bars outside your window and make a movement across it, backwards and forwards, with the right hand, just as if you were filing it away. She is as sharp as a needle, my Gabrielle," added the old fellow as proud as could be, "and she will understand what we want."

"Meaning a file, Antoine?"

"Meaning a file, Jacques."

"But how is she going to get it to us?" I said. "She can't bring it herself, and she could hardly ask Charlais to charge himself with such a thing for a prisoner."

"My son," said the old chap, "you know not Gabrielle. She is a man in determination but a woman in resource. All you have to do is to show her what we want, and then you may with safety and confidence leave the rest to her."

I'd been pretty well used to signaling aboard of Sir Philip's yacht, but I don't remember ever getting into such an excited state over signals on the *Swift* as I was the next day, standing at my open window and looking across the creek with a red silk scarf in my hand, waiting for the little peasant maid I'd loved so long. Would she come? Perhaps, having been disappointed the day before, she wouldn't feel like trying again. And yet, knowing that while her father lived he'd leave no stone unturned to try and get out of prison, she would hardly lose a chance of seeing for herself that nothing new was going on.

I'd been watching from just after breakfast until eleven o'clock or thereabouts, when at last the neat little figure with the pretty white cap and apron appeared at the edge of the creek, and the face turned full toward my window.

Now was the time! I got out the red scarf and waved it, like a flag, between the bars. I saw the girl give a start, then clasp her hands as though she were very glad—poor little soul—and then, standing quite still, she looked steady my way, so as not to lose a sign or signal I might give. I was just about to obey the orders Antoine gave me and make-believe file one of my bars, when I heard footsteps on the stone landing outside of my door. I had just time to stuff the red kerchief under my mattress and sit down on my box by the bed when the door opened and in came Charlais.

"I have brought you a visitor, Jacques," he said, "and as Monsieur wishes to have a private conversation with you, I shall lock you in together."

As Charlais spoke, the visitor followed him in. Sitting down on the chair, Monsieur Paul de St Rémy turned to me with the wicked smile, showing the sharp, tearing teeth at the corners, making him look like a hungry, grinning wolf.

"You are surprised to see me, Jacques Hamon?" he said, smiling broader and broader.

"I am surprised, Monsieur, and not at all pleased," I said. "It is hard, indeed, if even in prison one may not have freedom from intruders."

"Intruders, Jacques?" he said in the coaxing voice I'd heard before. "Are you so discourteous as to call me an intruder?"

"Yes, I am indeed," I said, not caring to mince matters. "Will Monsieur de St Rémy kindly state his business with me, and then do me the favor to leave me alone?" And saying this, I couldn't help looking impatiently at the window and wondering if Gabrielle was still waiting for me or had gone home.

The captain of the coast guard shook his head sadly with a sanctimonious sigh.

"Ah, Jacques!" he said. "So young you are, yet so vindictive! Truly you show a most unchristian spirit, and at a time, too, when I come to do you a service. But, alas! The world is very bad, very bad and ungrateful!"

He stopped there. I could see he wanted me to ask what service he wished to render me, but I was not going to speak just to pleasure him. Monsieur de St Rémy waited some time, then seeing I was keeping silence with a purpose, he said, "Would you know, Jacques, why I come to you this morning? Shall I tell you?"

"As Monsieur pleases," I said. "It is a matter I care nothing about."

A wicked flash came in those eyes of his that were so much too near together, but he spoke as soft and coaxing as ever when he said, "Well, Jacques, when I began to think over matters, I felt so sorry for you here in prison that I made up my mind to give you a chance of liberty—indeed, to set you free at once."

I knew very well that there was a lot behind this fair speech, and from his soft-soapy manner, I could tell the man was at his underhand tricks again. So I said, "Monsieur is, I see, bringing some more goods to market, but perhaps the price he asks is too high."

Then I smiled in my turn, and added, "Smuggled things, Maître Paul, fetch not always their full value, or at least so Simon and Jean would tell you."

At those words the man started to his feet with a savage oath, his face and voice changing all in a second. I meant him to drop that whitewash mask of his, and in his surprise and without thinking, he did so. Now he couldn't after this outburst begin soft and coaxing again, but would have to say straight out what the business was that he'd come for.

"I know not what you mean, Jacques Hamon," he said, his face belying his words—for he'd gone, all of a sudden, as white as a sheet. "I know not what you mean, but *n'importe!* These base insinuations of yours shall not hinder me in the purpose I had before me in visiting you today. Now, then, young man, do you wish to be free— to get out of prison?"

"What a question for Monsieur to ask!" I said.

"That means yes, I suppose," said Maître Paul. "Well now, if you choose, you can be free. I have influence; I can arrange matters so as to have you released, if—"

"Ah yes, Monsieur, now at last we are coming to it," I said. "If—"

"If you will just consent to sign a little paper which I have here." And Maître Paul took from his pocket a paper, and laying it down on the table, uncovered just the blank space at the foot of the page where the signing should be.

"I see there are pen and ink here," he said, and so there was, for Monsieur Valdac had told Charlais to bring me some.

"Now, Jacques Hamon," and Monsieur de St Rémy dipped my pen and held it out to me, "please sign, and I will sign after, as witness."

Well, I laid my hand on the paper, and I said very quietly and coolly, "Before I sign any paper of Monsieur's preparing, I must read every word of it."

"What nonsense!" exclaimed Monsieur de St Rémy, his temper rising at once. "What can a common fellow like you know about mere formalities like these?"

"As you please, Monsieur," I said. "Take the paper away with you; it does not interest me. As you observe, Monsieur, what can we common people know about such things?"

"Most men would do much more for their release from prison than sign a harmless paper," said Maître Paul.

"And I am no exception, Monsieur," I said. "But I must be

certain that what I am asked to do is honest and right and that the paper is harmless. Am I to read this paper of Monsieur's or no? If not, kindly take it, and leave me in peace."

"If you insist, I suppose you must see it," he said, very crossly and unwillingly. He allowed me to unfold it. Without letting myself be hurried or flurried, I took and read it right through. It was, as near as I could understand, made out to state that I'd not been sent with a document to bring over from England at all, that I'd not seen Monsieur Eustache Delmaine and knew nothing at all about him, that I'd merely landed in Brittany on my own affairs, and that therefore any paper produced in Paris and purporting to be the will of the late Monsieur Pierre de St Rémy was a forgery. For, if I had not brought it, it could not have been sent from England at all, as Monsieur Eustache was anxious to prove.

"And Monsieur wishes me to sign this?" I said, looking up at last.

"Yes, I do," said Maître Paul. "And just think of the reward you will have for just scribbling your name at the foot of that page— release from prison!"

"And if I refuse to sign, Monsieur, what then?" I asked.

"What then?" he repeated after me. "Then you can just rot in prison, and you shall, too! There will be no one to say a good word for you, no one to help you. Here—within these four walls—you remain till you die, Jacques Hamon, and not a friend of yours will ever be the wiser, or even know where you are buried."

"Very well," I said, "so be it then! At least my conscience will be clear; I do not mean to perjure myself for you or anyone else."

"I think you must be mad!" said Monsieur. "Surely, Jacques, this is not your final answer?"

"It is my final answer," I answered, feeling my anger rising and growing fast, and seeing in Maître Paul's dishonorable face that mine showed I was indignant and impatient. I think he was very glad (for he was beginning to be afraid of me) when the key turned again in the lock and my door opened.

It was Monsieur Valdac himself this time. As he stood on the threshold, he glanced from one to the other of us with those keen eyes of his and said much sharper than he usually spoke, "Monsieur le Capitaine, time is up."

My visitor snatched up his paper and put it into his pocket. He went a step or two toward the door, then turned his head and said, "Once more, and for the last time, I ask you, Jacques Hamon—will you do as I wish?"

"Not I, Monsieur," I answered.

"Then," he said, "say goodbye once and for all to the outside world, and imagine not for one moment that the Marquis or that brainless cat's-paw of a master of yours will raise a hand to help or liberate you. So now I assure—"

But to hear him speak like this of Sir Philip, my loved master, was too much for me. I sprang toward the open doorway, nearly overturning Monsieur Valdac, and before he could stop me, I laid hold of Maître Paul by the collar, just as he reached the stair, and I gave him one kick—the one I'd been dying to give him ever since I set eyes on him first. Well, my foot caught him quite unexpected, and he had what you might call a free passage down about a dozen stone steps. With a roar of rage, he was up in a moment and came rushing back at me with his eyes flaming and a dagger in his hand that he must have had up his sleeve all the time, to be ready in case he wanted it. But the old sergeant had recovered himself by now, and planting himself before me, he said, "Go into your cell, Jacques, and leave Monsieur to me."

I went into my room, and Monsieur Valdac stood in the doorway. When Maître Paul tried to pass him and come in, he said, very stiffly and politely, "Pardon, Monsieur, but time is up, and I cannot allow a longer interview with my prisoner."

Over the old sergeant's broad shoulder, the wicked mouth grinned and the wicked eyes glared at me, and between his gleaming white teeth, Maître Paul said, "If ever you cross my path again, Jacques Hamon, I'll shoot you as I would a dog."

"I fear you not, Monsieur," I said, "but look to yourself—there is danger lurking ever in each path of a life such as yours."

"Be silent, Jacques!" cried the old sergeant. "And as for you,

Monsieur de St Rémy, be so obliging, if you please, as to take your leave at once. *Bonjour*, Monsieur." And my jailor locked me in again and followed the visitor down.

I sat still a few moments, getting my breath, then I went back to the window and looked out for Gabrielle, but she was no longer there.

"Another chance lost!" I said to myself. "And I owe it to that scoundrel. The score against him is mounting up; I wonder when pay day will come!" And I tried to think what I'd do to my enemy if I had him in my power. I forgot who had said "Vengeance is mine, I will repay." Of course I couldn't know then that his triumph was, after all, to be a precious short one and that already the command of the Lord had gone forth, saying, "Thus far shalt thou come, but no further."

Chapter Eight

News and a Loaf

That night when all was quiet in the fort, the warder having made his last round, I took out the stone in the wall and told my friend Antoine all about Maître Paul's visit, and how, at parting, I had given him something to remember me by. I could hear the old chap chuckling on the other side of the wall as I told my story, but presently he said:

"Well, Jacques, we may laugh now, but when once you have left the prison behind you, you will be wise if you keep out of the man's way, for in this one thing—if in no other—I should say you may trust him to keep his word. If you cross his path, he will shoot you like a dog. You showed him you knew he was one of the smugglers; he must fear you for this, for were you at large, you could ruin his reputation—or what there is left of it—and he would lose his office under government. Then, too, he has reason to hate you for the part you have played in bringing over from England and safely delivering on this side the paper of which he was trying to get possession. And now, as if these things were not enough, you have made him your bitterest enemy by scorning his base proposals and finally by kicking him downstairs. So Jacques, my son, once clear of these walls, see that you expose not yourself to his vengeance. Of a truth, from what you tell me, it seems as if, had he but as little fear as he has conscience, he might be the greatest criminal known."

"Once clear of these walls, Jacques?" I said. "Why, you speak as though you were sure of our escape."

"And so I am," he answered. "I do not know whether it will be alive or dead, but somehow I mean to be outside the fort soon, and I think you mean the same, *n'est-ce pas*, Jacques?"

"*Mais oui, certainement*," I said. "By-the-by, Antoine, I was interrupted this morning by that villain's coming in just as I was beginning to show Gabrielle that we wanted a file. Tomorrow morning I must try again, and I hope to be more successful next time. Though, what the use is of telling her we need a file I do not know," I said, "for it is quite impossible that she should send us one."

"Be not too sure of that, Jacques," Antoine answered. "Love will find out a way of helping the beloved, and my faith in my little Rielle is firm. But now, *mon fils*, in preparation for our escape there is work to be done, and since we can only do it during the night, it would be well to commence at once."

"Yes, Antoine," I said, "you have only to direct, and I will obey."

"Good! You understand, do you not, that if we escape it must be through your window?"

"Yes," I said, "that is what we want the tool for—to file the middle bars."

"Precisely, but this is not all, nor even the first thing. The first thing will be for me to be able to get into your cell."

"Ah, true!" I said. "I had not thought of that." And, silly as it may seem, no more I had. "Then, Antoine, I suppose we must make a hole in the wall big enough to let you through. But if so, surely we can do nothing until the very night of our escape, for a large hole like that would be discovered at once by Monsieur Valdac or Charlais."

"Listen to me, *mon cher*," said Antoine. "Remember you how long it took to loosen and remove that one stone, and what hard work it was?"

"Yes, I remember," I said.

"And you know we had to manage so as to put the stone back in its place whenever we finished talking."

"Yes, *mon ami*, so that nothing should be noticed."

"Well now," said the old man, "stone by stone, we must do the same, until the space left in the wall is large enough for our purpose. The work of picking out the mortar and loosening the lumps of rock must be done little by little. We will take turns at it, passing the chisel to and fro, and working and resting alternately. Then, toward morning, we will put back the stones and fill in some of the loose mortar, so as to look natural. Your bed-head on one side of the wall, and mine on the other, will cover the loose stones and prevent anything being observed. Tonight we will commence our work of breaking through, and by the time everything else is prepared for our escape, this too will be ready."

For about three hours that night, Antoine and I toiled at dislodging the stones, and we managed, by picking out the mortar and working the stones up and down and from side to side, to partly loosen two of them. The bits of rubbish that tumbled down were all swept up, Antoine passing his through the wall to me, so that I could throw them out of the window right into the sea. His window—as I've said before—fronted on the land, and it wouldn't have done to throw bits where the sentry would be sure to see them.

The next morning, as soon after breakfast as I felt I could be safe from Charlais coming in, I took up my place at the open window, and this time I hadn't long to wait. In a very few moments came my little Gabrielle to the creekside, and, standing there, looked steadily and earnestly toward the fort, watching for the signal that was to be her instruction. So, first I waved my red flag for an instant, to show once more that I was acting under orders. Then I went to my door and listened, and hearing no footsteps on the stairs, I returned to the window and did the sign of the file on my middle bar. I did it for a good minute, I should say, and then left off, but remained there looking at her and wishing she could find a way to show me she understood. For I knew very well that this matter was important and that everything depended upon our having the right tool.

Well, for a bit the dear lass seemed to be thinking. Her hands were up to her face and her head bent down. Then, all of a sudden, she lifted her head, held out her left arm straight, like a bar, and with her right hand she sawed backwards and forwards across it.

"Bless you, dear heart!" I said and kissed my hand to her, so glad was I to see she understood. She waved her hand to me and was gone in a minute but left me with a lighter heart than I'd known for some time.

That night Antoine and I worked again at the wall, but we heard a noise on the stairs, or thought we did, and didn't go on after that.

The next day there was a big storm. The wind blustered and raved, the water came dashing up very high, and the noise was deafening. I stood at the window all the morning, but my dear girl didn't come to the creek.

"She's got her orders," I said to myself, "and she's trying to carry them out. She's a wise little woman not to run the risk of being noticed when there's naught to gain by it."

That night we worked, making as much noise as we'd a mind to, for what with the gale and the high tide, nothing short of a cannon shot could have been heard in the fort.

But the next day was quite calm. It was Sunday, and, as it happened, Charlais' Sunday out, so we had another soldier to bring us our meals. He wasn't half such a good-natured chap, nor yet such a chatterbox as Charlais, and didn't try to amuse us with the bits of gossip from the outside world that's so refreshing to us poor caged birds. We looked forward to Charlais' coming in the evening, and we were both of us longing special for him tonight, because, having been to his sister, the baker's wife, where Gabrielle was lodging, we might get scraps of news about her. Charlais would tell Antoine some things maybe, and me others, but the old man and me, we'd compare notes at night and talk over what we'd heard.

It was a long, long day; no service to go to and only one old book to read that Monsieur Valdac had found somewhere—a book with horrible pictures in it, of martyrs being killed in all sorts of awful ways that made one's blood run cold to look at. There wasn't much comfort to be gotten out of that book, as I soon found, and so I put it away and sat at my open window, looking out on the creek till supper came, and with it Charlais himself.

"Ah, Jacques," he said, as he put the little iron tray on the table, "you ought to be envious of your next door neighbor. Doubtless you would be if you knew what I had just taken to his cell."

"What is it?" I asked, trying not to seem so eager as I was feeling.

"A big loaf of new bread. The old prisoner's daughter made it herself in the bakery. The baker and his wife, my sister, are so fond of her, that there is nothing she would not be allowed to do. And when she begged so prettily, my sister told me, for permission to make a loaf of nice white bread for her father, they gave her leave. She has some special method of her own, I imagine," said Charlais, "and she does not wish others to know her secret, so she mixed her bread when she was alone in the bakery and baked it while my brother-in-law's ovens were still hot, after his own work was done for the week. Mademoiselle's loaf is long and slender, and looks nice and brown on the top, but somehow I fancy that *la petite boulangère* has made some mistake and that the dough did not rise as it should have done, for as I carried it from the village, it certainly felt much heavier than loaves of the same size usually do. However, you will see how it tastes, for I will ask the old man to send you a slice of his daughter's bread."

"Perhaps he will not wish to spare me any," I said, for the sake of saying something, but my thoughts were full of that file I'd asked for by signs, and I was thinking how clever it was of little Gabrielle to think of this way of sending it to us. For not a doubt was in my mind that it was the file, and nothing but the file, that made the loaf so heavy.

"*Holà oui!*" says Charlais in his odd Normandy French. "He will give you some with pleasure. He is not one of the greedy heart that keeps everything for themselves. But do you know, Jacques, that I have only told you half of my news?"

"Really, Charlais?" I said, thinking he would have nothing half so well worth hearing as what he'd just told me, but I was wrong.

"Yes," said the young soldier, sitting down while I ate my supper. "You know what a storm we had yesterday?"

I nodded.

"Well, in that storm, a fishing boat sprang a leak and foundered, about a mile off the coast. There were two men in her, and having cork jackets on, they managed to keep afloat till they were rescued by a yacht. The owner of the yacht proved to be English, and one of the kindest of men. He gave the poor fishermen dry clothing and plenty of good food and took the greatest care of them. One of the men landed close by here this morning and has a room in a house next door to my sister. He is a rough-spoken fellow but seems quiet enough."

"You did not happen to hear the name of the owner of the yacht?" I said.

"No, Jacques, but I know what the vessel was called. Ah, but the English have an uncouth language that we others cannot pronounce."

"And the name of the yacht was—?"

"Something like *Sveeft*," said Charlais, making a great face over it, as if it nearly gave him lock-jaw to try and bring out the word.

I bit my tongue and just kept myself from making a joyful exclamation—the thought of my dear master being so near was sweet, indeed!

"Were the fishermen who were saved strangers to the people here?" I asked.

"Well, not altogether, as it seems," answered Charlais. "There are rumors about their having been seen now and again lurking around the coast here and there. The man who is here now is called Simon, I think. The other's name I do not know."

I said nothing; I was thinking matters over. So it was Maître Paul's two men that had been rescued by the yacht, for as one was Simon, the other must be Jean. Oh, if only those men had known something about me, something they could have told my master! Here was I knowing a lot about them, having heard them talking and found out their smugglers' tricks, while they knew no more of me than if I hadn't been above ground at all. It was hard! Almost harder than I could bear. Sir Philip was so near, and yet I'd no chance of letting him know where I was!

"Quite a story, is it not, friend Jacques?" inquired Charlais, who was expecting me to say something.

"Yes, indeed, a very interesting tale, Charlais," I said. "And do you happen to have heard if Monsieur de St Rémy is in this neighborhood just now?"

"I heard in the village tonight that he has gone to Paris, Jacques, but he will be back again, *sans doute*, very soon."

"He is a restless person, this captain of the coast guards?" I said.

"*Holà oui!*" answered Charlais. "Only good people can be quiet and at rest, and he belongs not to that sort. But it is time I was going, Jacques Hamon, or I shall be scolded by M. le Sergent. Have you had all you want to eat and drink?"

"I thank you, yes," I said, handing him my tray with the empty plates and tin mug.

"Then goodbye, Jacques; sleep well. *Bonsoir—bonne nuit.*"

The light was put out, the door was locked for the night, and once more I was alone, but this time with plenty to think about. The hours passed quickly enough till just after midnight, when a tap near my bed-head showed me that Antoine was ready to begin work and to tell me what I was longing to hear—namely, his part of Charlais' story of the loaf.

Chapter Nine

My Share of That Loaf

"Jacques! Jacques Hamon! Is she not a treasure—an angel?"

These were the first words that reached me when I took out the usual stone. The other bits of rock being wedged in fairly all round, this one stone could be taken out well enough without moving the rest.

"Doubtless you are right, Antoine, but there are more shes than one in the world. Of which of them do you speak?" I said, for though I knew well enough, I wanted to hear what he would say.

"Why, *mon garçon*," he said, quite indignant, "you are indeed a dullard tonight. You, too, that pretend to love her! A fine love you are, to be sure, Jacques Hamon!"

The old chap was in good spirits—that was plain. His voice had lost the sad sound it had as of late and seemed to have a ring in it almost as if he were young again. The thought of getting away from this wretched place, and our planning together for it, had given him new life, or rather something to live for, which is often the same thing—at least so far as consequences go.

"*Ah oui, mon ami*," I said, "you speak of our little Gabrielle. Yes, ours—not yours alone—for as bad a love as you think me, I am not going to be cheated out of my share in this treasure—this angel."

"Forget not the condition, Jacques," said the old man. "When you have helped Gabrielle's poor old father to his freedom, then— and not till then—have you a claim."

"But meanwhile, Antoine, Charlais has promised me a share of something else."

"Of what, *mon fils*?"

"Why, what should it be but your beautiful new white loaf that he brought you only today; you see I have heard all about it."

The old chap laughed softly to himself at my remarks.

"It is well," he said. "A rash promise, perhaps, of Charlais'—but then he is rash. Yes, you shall have your share of the loaf, *mon garçon*, only complain not if you find it somewhat hard of digestion. Strange it should be so heavy," chuckled Antoine again, "for surely it has risen enough. Risen? *Ma foi, oui!* It has risen as high as the fort prison cells. Yes, my son, it is a fine loaf—solid and satisfying. *Tenez*, here is your share!"

And into my hand, stretched through the hole to receive it, he passed a small, hard, cold, iron tool—nothing more nor less than our coveted file.

"There was the crust of the loaf all round," says Antoine, "but that was all, unless indeed you can call this the crumb. And now, this very night, Jacques, you must begin to file your two central bars. There are six, are there not?"

"Yes, six," I said.

"Then, if we have the two middle ones out, that will leave us room to get through. You will begin tonight, Jacques?"

"*Mais certainement*," I said, "and what a good thing it is, Antoine, that there are no crossbars making a grating; that would give double work."

"You must file," continued the old man, "until the bars are all but cut through, so that five minutes more or a strong wrench will dislodge them entirely. On the night of our escape, these great stones in the partition wall come out for the last time, and our bars will come down to be replaced by other hands than ours."

He spoke as if all difficulties had already been overcome, and we were safe and free. I could see what energy and what spirit he must have had when he was young.

"Antoine," I cried, "so far, it is true, all goes well with our plans, but I have thought of another great difficulty, one which will be harder than all to meet."

"What is it, Jacques?" he said, very earnest and eager.

"*Mon ami*," I said, "have you considered what the walls of the fort are on this side? They are all of solid stone, and sheer down without a projection—a buttress—a parapet—to help us in our descent. Now, how are we, on getting out of the window, to reach the creek below?"

The old man didn't answer at once. It was a difficult question which he hadn't so much as thought of in his joy at getting the file and seeing his way through those bars. But at last he said, "Of course we want a rope, Jacques, and that is what we have not got, and cannot get either."

"*Mon camarade*, don't say that we cannot get it, at all events, until we have tried," I said, trying my best to speak encouragingly, for the poor old man's spirits had gone down with a run, and all his confidence was as though it had never been.

"It would be of no use asking Charlais, would it?" he asked presently in a pitiful voice.

"Worse than no use," I said, "for he is a gossip, and not only would he be unable to help us, but he would let out to Monsieur le Sergent or one of the others that we wanted a rope, and that would put an end at once to all hope of escape."

"Then, what would you advise, Jacques?" he said.

"Well," I said, "as Gabrielle has contrived so cleverly and so prudently in the matter of the file, I should now be disposed to ask her for a rope."

"And, pray, how is the poor child to convey to us a rope long enough to lower us from your window to the creekside?" asked Antoine, growing quite peevish in his distress.

"Courage, *mon ami!*" I said, putting an arm through the hole and patting him on the shoulder. "Remember you not how strong was your faith in Gabrielle's ingenuity and resources before? Well now, try them again—those resources—that ingenuity; prove once more what love can do!"

"She would do anything that could be done," said Antoine, "but even love cannot do impossibilities."

"We have yet to prove that this is an impossibility," I said.

"But," replied Antoine, "a fresh difficulty meets us at the very outset. How can we even let Rielle know that we want a rope?"

"I think I can manage that," I answered after thinking a minute.

"Tell me how," whispered the old man, leaning toward me with his ear close to the hole in the wall.

"You know I have writing materials here by the special permit of Monsieur Valdac, and I have been keeping a journal in English for my master, in case I ever get back to him? Well, I propose to make out of the large white sheets of paper given me, the letters of the word '*corde*.' These I shall show at my open window, one at a time, in the order in which they come, on the red background of the silk scarf."

"Good! A bright idea!" said Antoine. "But how do you propose to cut your letters? You have no scissors, have you? And mere written characters would not show at that distance."

"No," I answered, "I mean to get the letters all penciled out— half a meter in size—and then, when dinner comes up, I shall use my table-knife to cut them out. The knives here are not very sharp, but I shall spread the paper on the table and cut as near the penciling as I can."

So, having arranged our plans as far as we could, Antoine set to our usual task of picking out mortar and loosening stones, while I opened my window and did a bit of filing with my share of the loaf.

Next day, when Charlais had carried down the breakfast things, I took up my stand at the window as usual, for I didn't want, if I could help it, to miss the sight of my dear little girl. I wished to wave my red flag to show her all was well. I'd have been glad if I could, by any manner of means, let her know we'd gotten the file safe, and thank her for it, but this couldn't be, and she wouldn't expect it.

I hadn't been watching ten minutes before I saw not Gabrielle, but a man, coming from the village. He walked slowly along the cliff path by the creek, stopping now and again and glancing up at the fort towards my window. He was a rough, sailor-looking chap and walked with the lurching roll so many sailors get, almost as though they learned it from their ships. Watching as I was for Gabrielle, I grew quite impatient and cross seeing this stranger fellow dodging about.

"My little maid won't dare to look my way at all now," I said to myself, "and I can't make signals neither. Why, it might be one of Maître Paul's spies for all I know."

But even while I was grumbling and scolding away to myself, the little light figure I'd come to know and love so well came in sight, tripping over the short grass on the cliff to the side of the creek. As for the man, he turned, saw her coming, and stopped for her.

"How dare he? The brute!" I growled between my teeth. But I wondered more and more when I saw Gabrielle nod to him and then turn and look straight up at my window.

I knew well enough what she was looking for—the waving of the red scarf to tell her that nothing was amiss with her father. And when she saw no signal, but only me standing at the window, I thought she seemed anxious and troubled, for she drooped her pretty head in the way she'd done before, moving away a few steps and then coming back and looking up again, as though she was in fear something had gone wrong.

All of a sudden an idea seemed to come to her. She walked up to the place where the sailor chap was standing, and, taking him by the hand, she shook it long and hearty. Then she dropped it as though it was just a business matter and done with, and again glanced up at me.

"Well—if you ain't the brightest, cleverest little soul that ever was, I'd like to see one!" I said, and I got out my red flag and waved it once—twice—thrice—as usual. "You guessed why there was no signal, and you want to show me that the fellow's a friend. And now I think of it," I said to myself, turning away from the window, for I saw the two walking off together, "that may be Simon. Well, what I know of him ain't much to his credit, but if just now he comes from Sir Philip and in company beside with Gabrielle Claireau, it's as good as if he carried his certificate written out in full on his back."

Altogether, though I'd only seen my dear lass for a minute or two, I left my window that morning feeling as if our working from the inside of the prison wasn't all that was being done for our help. And the thought that perhaps my dear master wasn't far off, and that he as well as my little maid was on our side, was such a comfort to me that I longed to pull the stone out of the wall directly and cheer up poor old Antoine by telling him all about it. But of course this would have been dangerous, and so I tried to wait patiently till night might give me my chance of talking to him as usual.

As soon as Charlais brought my dinner, I took the knife and cut my letters out on the bare wood table. Being only a few, they didn't take long, and I'd time to hide them and eat my dinner before Charlais came back.

That night I filed longer than the previous night, and when I left off, the first bar was almost through at the top. As for the wall between our cells, it had now as many stones loosened as would, when taken out, make a big enough hole for Antoine to creep through. Our preparations were going as well as we could expect. If only we could get that rope, I knew I could contrive some sort of a ladder for Antoine to use, for he might not be strong enough, nor yet have the nerve to let himself down swinging from just a rope as I should do without thinking, through being used to all sorts of climbing and clambering up and down aboard ship and never knowing what it was to feel giddy.

The next day Gabrielle came alone to the creekside. After taking a careful look around to see that no one was watching, I spelled out *corde*. The letters must have been plain, for my little maid wasn't puzzled a bit; and what did she do to show me she understood but untie her apron and twist the strings together before she moved away.

The day after, though I was on the lookout as usual, I didn't see either her or Simon, but I spied a coast guard not far from the place and thought he was probably keeping them away.

That evening, when Charlais brought the supper, he said, joking, "What a pity it is, Jacques Hamon, that you have not a pretty girl to take an interest in you and bring you bread and lovely flowers!"

"A pity, indeed!" I said, wondering what was up now. "But no prisoners are so blessed as this, are they, Charlais?"

"*Holà oui!*" answered the young soldier. "Now, there's your neighbor—the old man next door. His daughter actually came to the fort today bringing some new laid eggs as a present for Monsieur Valdac and asked to be allowed to see her father. And when that was refused, she begged that a little bouquet of late autumn roses, grown in the baker's garden, might be taken up to him to show that his daughter thought of him and loved him. She spoke so prettily," added Charlais, getting quite sentimental over his story, "that our soft-hearted old sergeant could not refuse her, and he sent me up at once to Antoine with the bouquet, saying, 'At least no harm could possibly come of a gift like that!' And, of course, none could," said the wise Charlais.

"Harm? No, indeed!" I said to myself. "Good and only good—at all events to us poor prisoners." For in my mind I hadn't a shadow of doubt that by this nosegay of rose, my dear little maid was sending us an important message.

Chapter Ten

I Shot an Arrow Into the Air

"We have both stories to tell, is it not so, Antoine?" I said to my old neighbor through our speaking hole that night.

"Yes, indeed," he answered. "Tell me yours first, my son, for my story is a natural sequel to yours."

"But first, *mon camarade*," I said, "will you promise to give me a rose—just one out of your bouquet? Do not grudge me this; you cannot think how very precious it will be to me."

"Ah, so Charlais has told you of the gift I received, and you must have one of my roses?" said the old man. "Ah well, I too was a romantic fool once upon a time, but now—to business! And afterward you shall have the rose, your lovely *Gloire de Dijon*. You saw Rielle today?"

"I did, Antoine."

"Was the man whom you thought to be Simon with her?" (For, of course, I'd told him about seeing the sailor.)

"No, she came alone," I said.

"And—?"

"And I showed my big white letters, and she perfectly understood what we wanted."

"And, pray, how do you know that?" questioned Antoine.

Then I told him how Gabrielle untied her apron and twisted the strings, and he chuckled with pride and delight and said, "Ah, but that child of mine is a treasure! She has the brain of a savant, for all her innocent angel face."

"Now tell me, Antoine," I said, impatient to hear his part of the story, "what message did the bouquet of roses bring to you? For I cannot but think that it was sent for some special purpose."

"You are right, Jacques," answered the old man, "but it is a message that I understand not."

"For safety's sake, I suppose," I said, "Gabrielle had to be very careful, so that if her message fell into other hands, nothing would be known or even guessed."

"*Sans doute*. But you shall judge for yourself. Here is part of the message." And he slipped into my hand a piece of candle.

"This," he explained, "was right in the very middle of the bouquet, and quite concealed by the stems."

"How strange!" I said. "Now the other part of the message, Antoine!"

The old man handed me what felt like a long ragged strip of stiffish paper, like a bit torn hastily from some old exercise book.

"There is writing upon it," he said, "and it seems to be part of a sentence, just as if some child had written at dictation and a bit of the page had been torn off. Of course, the bouquet came before the lights were put out, so I learned the sentence by heart to repeat to you tonight, and these are the exact words, 'So, though he saw not any good reason for obedience, he still had faith and obeyed, every night putting a light in the open window just after midnight, for a space of three minutes.'"

"Had this writing been sent us without the candle, it would have been puzzling," I said, "but with the candle, it is plain enough, and we have nothing to do but have faith, as the writer says, and obey."

"But, Jacques, I cannot see how this can possibly have reference to our request for the rope; yet that is the only thing we need now to make our preparations complete."

"It is true," I answered, "that it does not seem to have anything to do with it, but there again the writing helps us. What does it say, Antoine? Please repeat it over again."

So the old man repeated the words, slowly and clearly, "'A light in the open window just after midnight for a space of three minutes.'"

"Good, Antoine," I said, "that will I do. Tonight it is too late, but tomorrow I will light the candle, put it in my window, and watch for what shall come. Gabrielle has some clever plan in her little head, of that we may be sure. But tell me, *mon cher*, is there nothing more on the paper—nothing save just this writing which you have repeated to me?"

"There was not another word," answered the old man, "but there was a strange mark at the end of the sentence that might have been an accidental slip of the pen, or it might have been made on purpose. But, *mon ami*, why question me? We have a candle, strike a light and look for yourself, and see what you can make of it. It is beyond me."

So I got out my tinderbox and soon had the candle alight.

Yes, there was the writing, looking like a child's hand (but that might have been feigned), and the sentence was just what the old man had been repeating, neither less nor more. But at the end of the sentence, there was the strange mark. I couldn't quite make it out, but it looked to me not unlike an arrow with a blunt head. I said so to Antoine, but he only sighed and shook his head over it, and I was just about as puzzled as he was.

"Well, Jacques," he said, "since we cannot understand, we must take the whole thing on trust. Light your candle after midnight tomorrow, and put it in your open window for three minutes. But blow the light out now, anyway; we have nothing more to learn from studying the writing, and the candle may not last us for all it has to do in the future if we waste it now."

So I put out the light, but not before Antoine had passed me the rose and I'd had a good look at it. A lovely, pale yellow, half-open bud it was, with a deep, fresh, cool heart of amber. Ah, what a treasure was that rose! But it wasn't till the light was out that I kissed it softly and breathed my darling's name over it and prayed God bless her. Then I hid it away under my pillow and took up the file and commenced filing—filing away for dear life—or what was dearer still, freedom; freedom for Gabrielle's father and for me.

I hadn't seen anything of our good sergeant for some days, but,

on the afternoon of the day following that on which we got the
roses, he came up. First he went in to see Antoine and afterward
paid me a visit. He sat down and chatted away very pleasantly for
some time, and at last I thought of a question I wanted to ask him.

"Can you tell me, if you please, Monsieur le Sergent," I
said, "whether Monsieur Paul de St Rémy is still in Paris or has
returned?"

"He is still away, Jacques, and since the man next in command
to him is a sot and idle as he can be, the coast guardsmen are just
having a holiday. There is neither order nor discipline among
them. I hear that at night they are constantly to be found drinking
themselves drunk at the tavern. Fine guardians of the shore they
are, indeed! But if Monsieur de St Rémy has no misgivings about
his men," Monsieur Valdac went on, "he seems to be really haunted
by the fear of you and Antoine escaping. About you especially," he
laughed heartily then continued, "he seems really anxious."

"Has Monsieur le Sergent then heard from the captain?"

"Yes, he writes me he is too busy to leave Paris but that he has
news from this neighborhood that a large English seagoing yacht
has been seen hereabouts off the coast, and that very likely my
prisoner Jacques Hamon may try to get away from the fort and
reach the vessel. Monsieur de St Rémy warns me that, if either of
my prisoners escapes, he shall hold me responsible. But bah! The
man is absurd! Look at these walls, those bars, the height of this
part of the building from the ground! Escape is simply impossible.
Or, even if it were possible for a prisoner to get out, he would only
be drowned in the sea. Yes, without doubt, it would be certain
death to attempt escape." And Monsieur Valdac looked at me very
earnestly and repeated the words, "Yes, certain death."

I said nothing to this. It wasn't for me to contradict my betters;
time enough when our getting clear away should give them the lie.

Monsieur Valdac went on, "The captain charged me to double
my precautions and to watch you narrowly; for—he assures me—
you are a very dangerous character."

"Yes, Monsieur, I confess," I said, "that to him I shall always be dangerous, and I am hardly so penitent as might be considered becoming in a prisoner, for having kicked Maître Paul downstairs."

Monsieur Valdac laughed.

"I have already replied to Monsieur de St Rémy's letter," he said, "telling him that, so far, neither of my prisoners has shown any impatience at his confinement, or made any effort to escape. I reminded him that had you wished to get free, you would have done so—or tried to do so, I should say—the day you rushed past me and kicked him downstairs. Of course," added the old soldier, "you could not have got quite away. That was—that is impossible, you know." And once more he put an emphasis on his words. "But still you might have gotten as far as the court or the outer hall and made a great stir and rumpus before we could stop you."

"Which would have been most foolish," I said solemnly.

"Quite so, Jacques," said Monsieur Valdac. "I am glad to hear you speak so sensibly of any attempt at escape."

"Pardon, Monsieur! It is not so; Monsieur le Sergent misunderstands. The foolishness would be in making a stir and rumpus. Those things, if done at all, should be done quietly."

"I like not to hear you speak thus, Jacques," answered the old sergeant. "Still, I hold you an honest man, with all due respect to the opinion of Monsieur de St Rémy. If you will now give me your word of honor that you will not try to escape, I can trust you and shall not further disquiet myself on your account."

I shook my head.

"Monsieur," I said, "I will make no such promise, for if I had a good chance of escape this moment, I should take it. Monsieur le Sergent is, however, right in thinking me an honest man. I am this— and in nothing do I prove it more than by refusing to perjure myself. Monsieur will doubtless remember what I said to him before on the subject, and in no sense have my feelings changed since then."

"In that case I must charge Charlais to be very careful, and I myself must be strict—ah, so strict!" said the kind old man, doleful and sad at the thought, trying to look severe and failing so entirely that he nearly made me laugh outright. "Nevertheless, *mon garçon*," he said, "I cannot but respect your candor, and while I regret that you cannot reconcile yourself to a quiet acceptance of your lot, I do not blame you for wishing to be free. But never yet," and my jailor drew himself up, holding his head very high, "never yet has Nicholas Valdac allowed personal feeling to interfere with duty, and he will not begin to do so now." And with this awful threat, Monsieur le Sergent took his leave, and I heard a chain put up, as well as the locking and bolting of my door.

That night, soon after twelve o'clock, I lit my candle and put it in the open window. There wasn't a breath of wind, so it didn't flicker. It burned quite steady and bright for the whole of the three minutes while I sat there watching, but nothing happened, and at last I got up, put out the light, told Antoine that I'd seen and heard naught, and set to work filing, for there was still a good bit of this left to do.

The next morning Charlais came in looking very cheerful, and from this I made sure he'd something to tell, for I do believe nothing gave him such pleasure as a good long gossip, though he never said spiteful or unkind things, as so many gossips do.

"Good morning, Charlais!" I said. "Your face is full of news. Let me have it, please."

"*Holà oui!*" he said. "One of the coast guardsmen has already called in here this morning, and he says that their lieutenant has received a letter from Monsieur le Capitaine to tell him to keep strict watch for spies and deserters, whether landing on the coast or leaving it for any vessel outside. As he offers a reward to any of the men on duty who catch a spy or a deserter, they will perhaps now begin to be vigilant. I only wish I had a chance to earn extra pay like that!" added Charlais. "But we poor fellows in the fort are tied by the leg."

I did not answer. Charlais' news had thrown a dark shadow over our prospect of escape that seemed brightening just before. How in the world was our signaling to go on with those coast guards prowling about, diligent all of a sudden, in hope of filling their pockets? And how was Gabrielle to get that rope to us, without which all we'd done already was useless? Were Maître Paul's words to come true after all—that we should rot in prison?

I hardly know how the next few days went; I was so downcast that I didn't seem to take any interest in anything. If I had any hope, I used it all up every night in trying to keep up the spirits of poor old Antoine, who was worse than me. Still, though I couldn't see much use in it, I regularly put the light in my window after midnight, when the warder had made his round. So far nothing had happened. When I looked out in the daytime, I didn't see Gabrielle nor Simon, only a coast guard or two, prowling like watchdogs up and down the cliffs.

But one night, when the candle had burned down so low that I hardly thought it could last for another time, I was sitting watching as usual when something, all of a sudden, came whizzing in at the window over my head and fell on the floor at my feet. I picked it up and saw it was an arrow, blunt headed, with a strip of paper wound round it and a thin string fastened to it. There was writing on the paper, "When the arrow reached him he waved the red flag once, then blew out the light, and began to haul in."

In an instant I got the red kerchief and waved it through the bars. With the light behind it, it was sure to be seen. Then I blew out the candle and began to haul in my line, and a strange kind of fishing it was. After a minute or two of hauling on the thin string, I came to a knot, and then to a thicker cord. After that I went on pulling away, and then came another knot and a stout cord, and then—again, after a while—a thick, strong rope. All the long line, save only the first thinnest twine, was soaking wet, showing that it had come through the creek, as I hauled in. Of course the thin string had been shot through the air with the arrow.

I don't know how long it took to haul in all that lot of cord and rope, but it was a good while, for as I hauled I coiled it, untying the knots, and put each size of cord in a flat coil by itself. Then, when all was neatly coiled and fastened, I tore open a bit of my mattress and put my coils away among the straw, and no one would have guessed they were there.

Then I told Antoine all about it, and together we rejoiced over the rope. But the old man was puzzled about who could have shot the arrow, for he says Gabrielle has no notion of such things. Then I thought of Simon. It was likely enough that during his voyages he'd often had occasion to shoot wild fowl and duck and such for food, and firearms and powder and shot wasn't cheap enough for poor men to buy, so perhaps he'd had some practice with bow and arrow.

But how it was that the coast guard didn't prevent the doing of it was more than either of us could account for. That was one of the things which remained to be explained when Antoine and I had made our escape.

After telling Antoine all about the rope, I lit my tiny end of candle again to show him the writing, and then we saw what I hadn't noticed before—some words written at the back of the paper. I read them out.

"'After this, he did nothing further until he heard from his friends, but he kept a careful watch every morning, until one day he saw something flying that was not a bird.'

"These are our orders, Antoine," I said, "and we can understand all that it is needful for us to know. We have friends who are working for us; let us do nothing rash, but be patient, trusting to those who know better than we can the right time to act."

"Yes," said the old man, with a sigh that was almost a groan, "you are right, *mon ami*; there is nothing for it but patience."

Chapter Eleven

How We Did It

It was good that we'd made up our minds to be patient, for patience was very needful. It did seem hard when—so far as we knew, we'd gotten all that was necessary for getting away—we still had to wait. But we could only believe that those outside had a better chance of seeing how things really were, and we felt we could trust them to give us sailing orders so soon as they found the wind fair for us.

But life seemed wonderfully dull, now that there was nothing to do, and the time hung so heavy on our hands that we'd have been thankful for any sort of work, if we could have gotten any.

Our only bit of change and pleasure was when that dear, good-natured fellow Charlais brought us scraps of news from the world outside, or Monsieur Valdac paid us a visit. It was from one of them—I don't rightly remember which—that I learned how Maître Paul was still away in Paris, though he'd been expected home some time ago. Also there was a rumor that he had got into some difficulties there, though what was the nature of them didn't seem to be known. Charlais, too, now and then, brought us tidings of Gabrielle, and mentioned Simon too, who he said was often out fishing and did not always come home, even at night.

The weather was mild still, one of those long, late seasons, carrying brightness and warmth right into November. This kind

of weather is not at all uncommon, I've understood, in that part of
France.

Morning after morning I'd kept careful watch at my window,
but I had seen nothing, save that twice Gabrielle walked on the cliff
by the creek, and, pretending to blow her nose, waved her white
kerchief to me. Once I saw Simon spreading out a big net as if to
dry, stopping in his work to talk to a coast guardsman as he passed.
I could see they were laughing together and seemed quite good
friends, which I was astonished at, but that also was one of the
things that came to be explained later.

Well, time passed, and I'd begun to fear that the orders we
were awaiting would never come at all, or they wouldn't come till
winter was upon us, making a long swim, especially for Antoine,
nearly impossible. And yet the only way we could escape was by
swimming down the creek, out to sea, and getting to the island.
Simon might perhaps have met us outside the creek with his boat,
but now, since these special orders had come from the captain, the
coast guards were on the watch along the front of the fort for boats
coming and going, and their own was always at hand to put off and
follow so that we couldn't have much chance. Long since I'd made a
rope ladder to help us in getting down, first from my window to the
cliff, and then from the cliff to the water. The rope ladder was a big
thing, and I hardly knew where to hide it; indeed, I couldn't have
kept it out of sight at all if our prison had been like some, where the
cells and everything in them is inspected often. But Charlais was
a very easy going chap, having no idea of strictness, and Monsieur
Valdac didn't know much more about it. So, as long as we were
careful to keep our cells nice and clean, washing the stone floor
every other day and having all neat and tidy, no one interfered with
us. The rope ladder hidden in my straw mattress was never seen,
and our plans were not suspected.

Well, we were almost in despair with waiting—poor old Antoine
and me—when one dull, heavy morning, as a wind from the land
was blowing a mass of dark clouds seaward, I was watching as usual
at my window when I saw Gabrielle running along, and with her,

little Narcisse, the baker's eldest son. The child had gotten a great big kite, and she was showing him how to fly it. As she ran lightly along the cliff, she turned her head my way and made a sign toward the kite as it sailed on the wind, its front opposite my window.

The words came back to me, "Something flying that is not a bird!" Here it was, then—the promised signal! The hour of our deliverance was at hand at last! But what my surprise was I couldn't tell anyone, when, on the kite's white front, printed in great black letters, I read some English words, "Tide turns midnight. Strike out with ebb. Land on rock, seaward side."

For a minute I could hardly help shouting for joy, but the next thing I did was to burst out sobbing—a dry sobbing without a tear. I'd been hoping against hope so long, and now at last here came the message we'd been waiting for, and signed, too, with my dear master's own double P, standing for his name of Philip Penreath.

But I was brought to my senses by seeing Gabrielle pausing while the child ran on with the kite—pausing and gazing my way, waiting for some sign that I'd read and understood.

"It's all right, my love, my darling!" I said, as I waved the red scarf once at the window. She turned away satisfied and followed the boy Narcisse. A coast guard, just returning from his *déjeûner*, came in sight, but he wouldn't know a word of English, and if he did, he would never guess that a child's toy had a message for a prisoner in the fort, so we were safe enough. Of course I couldn't wait till night to tell Antoine my news, for we'd both have to be ready and waiting to start directly when the fort was quiet. So I wrote down as short as I could what I'd seen and the kite's message. When Charlais had taken away our dinner things, and I knew we shouldn't see anyone again for some time, I pulled out our talking stone (as we called it), and dropped the note into his cell. I put back the stone at once, but the mortar being out, I could hear every sound inside when my ear was near the wall. I heard the paper rustle, and I caught the murmur of his voice as he read to himself what I'd written. Then he gave a great big sigh, as if he was throwing off a load from his poor old heart, and he said, "Thank God! Oh, thank God for His mercy!"

When Charlais came up with my evening meal, he said to me, "Ah, Jacques, more news! But perhaps not so pleasant as what I brought you lately."

"What is it, Charlais?" I asked.

"M— le Capitaine is expected home tonight," said the young chap. "Ah, I thought you would look pleased when I told you that, and you do," and Charlais laughed gaily.

"And at what time is he supposed to arrive?" I asked, trying to seem as if I didn't much care.

"I know not the exact hour," answered Charlais, "but from what the lieutenant said, I should say any time between eleven and two."

"If we do get off tonight, it'll only just be in time," I said to myself when Charlais left me. "Let that man settle here again, and there's no chance for us."

During the time between Charlais' last visit and the round of the warder at midnight, I got everything ready. And first, one end of a piece of strong rope I knotted firmly about two of the sound bars in my window. Then I fastened the rope ladder in the same way but let the other end of it hang down outside. I slipped the cold chisel into one trouser pocket, but the file was too heavy to risk swimming with, so I hid it under the bed. Then I got one of the hanging nails out of the wall and ran it into the keyhole in my door to hamper the wards and make delay, in case anyone should take it into his head to look us up before morning. Then, when all was quiet in the fort, we took out the loose stones in the wall between the rooms, and very softly and quietly Antoine crept into my cell through the opening. Both of us had left off our coats and boots, and our caps remained hanging on the nails. Antoine was stripped to his shirt and trousers and socks, and I was the same, except that I had on an old knitted jacket over my cotton shirt. Antoine glanced through my open window; I'd taken the two bars out, and it seemed almost like freedom to look through the wide space that was left between them.

"A dark night," he said. "There may be a storm soon. It is warm, too—just the right weather for us."

For all we'd done we hadn't needed light. We were so used to working in the dark that it was like second nature to us.

"Now," I said to Antoine, "you are to go first. Put the loop of this single rope around you under the arms, but descend by the ladder. Then, should you feel giddy or slip, the rope will prevent your falling. As soon as you reach the ledge of rock running around the fort on this side, undo the loop so that the rope hangs free. I will then unfasten the ladder from the bars and drop it down to you so that we can use it in descending the cliff to the creek."

"But you?" said Antoine. "How will you get down from your window?"

"I? Oh, I can let myself down by the rope easily enough," I said. "I am a sailor, you know. Now, *mon camarade*, are you ready? For we must not lose a moment."

"I am ready," said Antoine.

I helped him up to the window, and then he turned, facing me, and began to descend the ladder, rather slowly and timidly at first, but quicker and firmer presently. I looked over and watched him and seemed to breathe more easily when I saw him set foot on the strip of rock, which, though it was narrow, just gave him foothold. Then I undid the fastening of the ladder and dropped it, and he caught it as it fell and walked a few steps further along the ledge to where the space outside the wall of the fort was a bit wider. I came down the rope quite easily and quickly, steadying myself by one foot twisted in it, feeling safe and comfortable enough. Then I followed Antoine and began looking for a firm bit of rock sticking out and the right shape to loop the ladder over. After a minute or so I found one and got the fastening cords, as well as the top rung of the ladder, over and around it.

As for the rope I'd come down by from the window, I was obliged to leave that hanging, just as we should have to leave the ladder, too. But, after all, it wouldn't much matter if the people of the fort—when we'd gotten away—did see how we'd done it. Antoine was more confident this time and went down the rope ladder almost as nimbly as I could have gone myself. I waited till I heard a splash,

and then I followed the old man. I could just see, as I got nearer the
bottom, a silver speck on the dark water, his head being as white
as snow. Another moment and I'd plunged in and was swimming
close beside him. The tide had turned, so we were carried out swiftly
toward the sea. So far, it was easy enough, but once out of the creek,
there was a belt of surf running all around and breaking on a reef.
What wind there was came from the land, so the breakers weren't
high at all, but still, it wasn't easy to swim in. Poor Antoine began to
breathe heavily and did not seem to be able to manage.

"You had better leave me, Jacques," he said, gasping as he
tried to keep his head above water. "Save yourself. Why should we
both drown?"

"Neither of us will drown if I can help it," I said. "Now, Antoine,
turn over on your back; float and rest. See how the generous sea
supports you! So—don't move; these little waves are nothing, and
we shall be out of them directly. Don't be afraid; I won't let you go
under, *mon ami.*"

I think my being so confident gave him courage, for after a
minute or so he said, "I am better, Jacques; I can go on now." And
together we struck out once more for the island. Thrice we had
to stop while the old man rested. I kept one hand under his neck
while treading water so we wouldn't drift out of our course with the
current. Altogether, we must have been in the sea about half an hour
by the time my feet touched land, and I dragged my old comrade
out of the water. When I did so and laid him on one of the flat
rocks, he lay there at first like a dead man. I went down on my knees
beside him and chafed his hands and rubbed his chest and neck,
and it was while I was doing this that the first flashes of lightning
from the storm that had been gathering all day lighted up sky and
sea and shore. On account of Antoine's being so done up, we'd been
obliged to land on the flat rocks facing the creek instead of following
the instructions given us to land on the other side. But when the
flashes began to make everything as bright as day every now and
again, I felt it would be madness to stay here where we might be
seen from the shore; so, as Antoine was getting better, I said to him,

"As soon as you feel able to move, *mon ami*, we must get around to the other side of the island; here we are not safe a moment with this lightning playing about us and our enemy on the lookout."

Antoine scrambled up as quickly as he could and, with my help, managed to creep around over the rocks till we reached the sea-facing side. There, after some little searching, I found a hollow, which was almost a cave, that would give us shelter from the storm. It was found at just the right time, for the flashes were brighter than ever, the thunder rolled overhead, and a heavy rain was falling now. The air, too, was growing colder. A thunderstorm at this season is a rare thing, and when it does come, it nearly always brings a change of weather, and we in our wet clothes could not but feel chilled to the very bones, so long we'd been in the water. However, we crept in under cover of the roofing rock, where neither wind nor rain could reach us, and found some soft, dry sand in which we made holes to lie in; and being so worn out with all we'd gone through, we soon fell asleep, and I did not wake till daylight in the morning.

Chapter Twelve

The Last of Maître Paul

I cannot be sure that I should have awoke even then, but for a song that I seemed at first to hear in my dreams, and that woke me at last. It was a hoarse, gruff voice droning out an old Normandy ditty that ran something like this—

Our William was a conqueror bold;
Vive la Normandie!
His valiant deeds in song are told;
Vive la Normandie!
He landed firm on Angleterre,
With all his noble hommes de guerre,
Vive la Normandie!

I started up from my sand bed. The old man was still sound asleep with the morning light on his weary face. He looked ill, I thought; his cheeks were flushed with fever and his lips parched.

Very cautiously I crept to the opening of our little cave and peeped out, and there, it might be about twenty yards away, I saw a fishing boat bobbing up and down at anchor. The one man sitting in the boat had some lines overboard and was singing as he fished. I couldn't see his face, the way the boat was turned, but I was afraid it might be someone Maître Paul had set to watch the island, in case of my having escaped to it. So I hardly dared more than snatch a glance his way for fear of being seen. But suddenly he turned his head, and I recognized Simon, and at the same moment, looking out into the open beyond him in the offing, what should I see but the great white wings of the *Swift*! Yes, I couldn't be mistaken; there wasn't another vessel as could compare with her. And as I caught sight of the yacht with the sunlight flushing her sails, I could have laughed aloud if I'd not been crying like a baby at the time.

But the man Simon, in his look my way, had caught sight of me, and it was plain he had his orders. First he hoisted a little flag to the top of his mast and let it down again, then he pulled up his anchor and lines, all in a twinkling, and chucked them under the seat, while he got out his oars. And then, turning, he headed for the island, keeping well behind, so as not to be seen from the shore.

"Antoine, wake up!" I said, taking the old man by the shoulder and shaking him a little. He opened his eyes and looked at me, but there was no meaning in his look, and he only answered with a groan.

"Antoine," I said, thinking to rouse him, "there is a boat to take us to our friends and freedom. Listen, *mon camarade*, is this not what we have been praying for?"

But the answer he muttered with those dry lips was not one I could understand.

By this time Simon had caught hold of the rock with his boat hook and pulled in close.

"Make haste," he said, "and let us get away. There will be a stir on shore directly when you are missed. I should have met you here last night, but a corvette was cruising about, and I was afraid of taking you off in sight of her. I should have roused you before, but the yacht has only just come in sight, and it would not have been safe to start till we saw her."

"The old man is ill," I said. "Help me lift him into the boat."

Antoine didn't stir a finger as we lifted him and laid him flat down in the bottom of the boat, where Simon threw a pilot coat over him.

"Now," said our boatman, "take an oar if you can, Jacques
Hamon, for if I am not much mistaken, we shall have the captain
out after us directly; he'll be after me as well as you. He was to come
back from Paris last night, and every yard we can get farther away
from the shore and nearer to the yacht is that much clear gain and
may mean life to us all."

I seized one oar and Simon the other. He had already spread
a sail to catch a faint breeze that blew from the side. A few strong
strokes and we'd left the island behind us and were fairly on our way
to the yacht. Our faces being turned toward the shore in rowing, I
could see the fort and the creek and the waves dashing up around
the jutting-out cliff. It really seemed as if the night we'd just been
through must be nothing but a dream after all—a dream that I
should wake out of soon, to find myself in prison again.

Question after question came up in my mind, and I turned
to Simon to ask them, but he stopped me short and said, "Do not
talk, Jacques Hamon! Save your breath for rowing. Look there!"
and he nodded in the direction of that part of the shore just below
Monsieur Paul de St Rémy's house, and a little to the left of the
château of Monsieur Eustache Delmaine.

I followed Simon's nod, and the next stroke of my oar sent the
boat spinning along. Indeed, I hardly knew what I was doing. For
there, just pushing off from a little wooden jetty belonging to the
coast guard station, was a long boat, manned by six men, and in the
stern, steering the boat, sat Monsieur le Capitaine himself, leaning
forward as if to speak to his rowers and hurry them on.

"There—see you?" muttered Simon. "And mind, Jacques, if
we are taken, it means death to us all three—to you as spy, to the
old man as traitor, and to me as deserter to the English. Now for a
pull!" And as he spoke, the stout old smuggler put his back into the
rowing, and so did I—sending the tub along through the water, as I
should say she'd never been sent before.

For a bit we held our own, but as we got farther out, and there
was more sea, the bigger, better manned boat had the best of it.

Simon and I toiled at our oars. He looked around now and again
to see how the yacht lay and steered accordingly with the bow oar.
On we went dashing through the water, the spray breaking over us,
as we shoveled her along—for I can't call our mad rowing anything
else. But still the coast guard boat, with the six fresh rowers, crept
nearer and nearer. It was close enough now—in spite of our doing
our utmost—for me to see Maître Paul's face and the cold cruel
smile that showed those tearing teeth that were so like a dog's, or
more still a wolf's.

"Oh, Lord!" I murmured. "Surely it can't be Thy will that after all
we've passed through we should fall into this man's hands at last!"

It was an unrighteous prayer—if it could be reckoned a prayer at
all. The Lord had been so good—so very good to us—I might have
trusted Him a bit longer. But the Almighty was too pitiful to punish
me for my faithlessness. His answer came quick—quicker than such
a cry deserved.

The pursuing boat, by a few strong strokes, had gained on
us several yards, and now Maître Paul stooped down and took
from the bottom of his boat a gun. Then he stood up, got it to his
shoulder, and aimed it at me. He seemed to be just waiting for
a steady moment between the bobbles of the sea, when, all of a
sudden, I heard my master's clear voice ringing out over the water,
"That's it, gunner! Let her go! Spoil his aim for him, but fire wide.
We only want to save our Jack."

Then a great crash and boom came thundering across the sea,
and there was smoke and a big splash to our right, not very far
from the pursuing boat. The coast guard craft was rocking and
lurching, as the men, startled, thinking they were sinking, jumped
up from their places. But when I glanced around again, the big
boat was steady, Monsieur Paul's seat at the stern was empty, and
the fellows were lying on their oars and peering over the sides of
the boat. Simon and I looked at each other, and the man nodded.
"Overboard," he said. "It is plain enough how it happened. He was
standing up to aim at you, Jacques, when the noise of the big gun

and the splash and smoke startled him, and he must have lost his balance and gone over. It is nothing. He will come up again; he is a strong swimmer." Even as Simon spoke, we saw a dark head bob up and a dozen arms outstretched to pull the captain in. He looked very like a drowned rat, yet he had spirit or spite enough left in him to shake his fist at us, but we only laughed at this, knowing that he was helpless, his gun having gone to the bottom when its owner went overboard.

By this time the *Swift* was close to us, and as I glanced up I saw my dear, dear master looking at me over the ship's side, and next to him—the greatest wonder of all—my little Gabrielle, her face all tears and smiles, and bless me if I know which there was more of.

"Now then, look alive there, boys!" cried the big voice of the sailing master. "Get our people aboard! Our gun has brought those rascally French cruising about from all parts, and we shall have the corvette down on us if we don't get away. She's only just round the corner of the cliff now."

We handed up the old man, and the sailors took him in strong, tender arms and carried him below, where Gabrielle followed him. Then Simon got on board and saluted Jean, who was grinning from ear to ear and talking his Normandy French at the top of his piping voice. And, last of all, I went up—rather stiff and lame. The next thing I knew was Sir Philip taking me by both hands, shaking them and saying, "My brave, trusty lad! Thank God, I've got you back!"

And then my dear master turned away with a bad cold, and I did a lot of swallowing before I could get down a marble in my throat.

Then the order was given to crowd on all sail, and in five minutes more the *Swift* was heading for dear old England, leaving the French coast and the dodging, meddlesome, little busybodies of French vessels far behind.

My dear master, he wouldn't hear nor tell anything until I'd had a bath and a change and a good meal, and then he called me into his private cabin, where I looked around for the Marquis. Sir Philip saw the look, and he said, "The Marquis is not with me, Jack. When we found you'd been made prisoner, I took him back to England. It would not have been safe to have him onboard when we were cruising about. You see, if the French had taken us prisoners, that is all they could well have done to us, whereas the Marquis would most likely have lost his life, and the risk was one too great to run. I can tell you, my lad, I have been backward and forward a good many times, never missing a chance of finding out something about you. But all my efforts were in vain until one stormy night—"

"You saved two Normandy fishermen as their boat foundered, Sir Philip?"

"Ah," said my master, "you heard the story?"

"That much of it, Sir Philip," I answered. "But, of course, as those fisherfolk didn't know me, they could tell you nothing."

"Nay, there you are mistaken, Jack," said my master. "Simon gave me information about you which was of the utmost importance, for it showed me into whose hands you had fallen. Ah, my lad, you look surprised," Sir Philip went on. "Do you remember Monsieur Eustache Delmaine giving you a receipt for a certain document that was sent to him by your hand?"

I stared with all my eyes. How on earth did my master come to know about that?

"Why, yes, Sir Philip," I said. "When Maître Paul—I mean Monsieur de St Rémy—was searching me for the will, he found it in my pocket. He crumpled it up in his anger and disappointment and threw it down on the floor. I'd have picked it up, but my hands were tied behind me."

Sir Philip took out his pocket-book, opened it, and handed me a paper—the very same—only crumpled, torn, and with dirty finger marks all over it.

"Oh, I have it now, Sir Philip," I cried. "When I was sitting in the dark in Maître Paul's house, I heard a man come to visit him in the next room, and I knew the gruff voice—as soon as the man spoke— as one of those smugglers I'd heard talking in the cave when they were waiting for their master. The man was Simon, Sir Philip, and he must have picked up that paper."

"By Maître Paul you seem to mean Monsieur de St Rémy," said my master. "But what is this you say about smugglers? Surely the captain had nothing to do with them?"

Then I began my story from the time of leaving the yacht and told it all, much as I've told it now. At some of it Sir Philip laughed, and at some his eyes were wet, and he looked at me kind of pitifully. And when I told him about Gabrielle and my dreams, and the drawings, and the finding out that my neighbor in the prison was her father, he was so pleased that it touched and moved me, for I might almost have been one of his own family or friends, instead of only a sailor aboard his yacht. Sir Philip, on his side, made some things clear to me that were not so before. I learned that, during the latter part of our imprisonment, when any signals to me were to be made, Simon would attempt to engage the attention of the coast guard on duty, taking him off to a cozy *déjeûner*, or dinner, entertaining him royally at Sir Philip's expense, and thus leaving the coast clear.

And now not much of this story remains to be told. Poor old Antoine was very ill for a day or two, and we were half afraid we might lose him. But God was good to us, and Gabrielle and I, we nursed our dear old father back to life. Yes, our father—not hers alone—for when I came to talk with my dear little girl, I found she'd no more forgotten me than I her. Since we loved each other, and there really didn't seem to be anything to wait for, we were married just as soon as Antoine was well enough to give away my bride.

I mustn't forget to say, though, that both the Marquis and Monsieur Eustache Delmaine behaved most generously, and our pretty home is furnished from top to bottom with what they gave me.

I don't need to say how happy we are; we both think we never knew how happy we could be till now. But often, when the wind is raving at night around the snug house where I live, when I am not at sea in the *Swift*, the three of us—for of course *le Père* lives with us—talk over those dreadful times now past and of all we went through. We don't regret anything because we believe that all the anxiety and trouble and danger drew us nearer together than we could ever have been without them. I say sometimes to Gabrielle, that the *bon Dieu*, to provide for me the one woman in all the world who could make me perfectly happy, sent me to prison in a Breton fort. And then my wife laughs and says, "Ah, *mon cher*, that imprisonment was nothing compared with what thou now shalt have, for I will be to thee no indulgent jailor, like old Valdac or young Charlais, and from the prison of my heart there is no escape for thee, beloved, by land or by sea."

But all I answer to my new jailor is, "Amen, my darling, so be it!" And it is.

The End

More Books from The Good and the Beautiful Library

Dawn
by Eleanor H. Porter

Little Men
by Louisa May Alcott

A Girl of the Limberlost
by Gene Stratton Porter

Up From Slavery
by Booker T. Washington

www.thegoodandthebeautiful.com